Eligible Best Friend

MARIE JOHNSTON

LE PUBLISHING

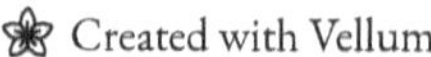 Created with Vellum

To all the other women in town, Ford Monroe's a player. To his ex, he's a failure she doesn't want around their kid. But to me, he's my best friend. The single dad and I both work as paramedics and are partners on the job. Dating isn't worth ruining the best relationship I've ever had, no matter how hot he is.

But when my ex-fiancé comes to town to woo me back and Ford's ex-fiancée claims he's a poor role model for his son, Ford has an idea. An idea so crazy it might just work to get both our exes off our backs.

We're only supposed to pretend to date, but it's not long before I want the real thing. Yet when Ford's life gets rear-ended, the romance growing between us gets put on life support. He has to put his son first, and I'm done changing bandages on my heart for a guy.

Eligible Best Friend was previously published as *Shock* in K. Bromberg's Everyday Heroes World project. Some details have been changed, but the story is still the same.

One

Lia

"And then he did this thing with his tongue—"

The woman, whispering at full volume to her friend while picking out condoms and lube, glances over at me. Her face flushes, and she bites her lip. I can't tell if she's embarrassed or about to come from the memory of the guy with the tongue.

Her friend shoots me an irritated look, but it's not as if I knew they'd be in their yoga pants and moisture-wicking tees, taking their time picking out his-and-hers KY and trading hookup stories. Aren't there bars for that? This is the personal hygiene aisle of a grocery store.

"Excuse me." I try to step around her to grab a box of sport tampons because I refuse to admit a tampon is the biggest thing I've had in my vagina for a year.

Her eyes sweep down my outfit, snagging on the Star of Life on my chest. I'm used to getting second glances when I'm out in my EMT uniform, a white polo and my black tactical pants. I try not to run errands in my work clothes, but I have a lunch meeting tomorrow I'm trying not to think about and getting to the store after work is always iffy. I never know what bodily fluids I'll encounter during a shift.

"Are you with Fargo EMS?" The woman who had been gushing about her sexcapades faces me with a greedy glint to her hazel eyes.

I don't mean to, but I glance down at the emblem on my shirt that reads *Fargo EMS*. "Uh, yep."

Her grin widens and she leans forward so far that I take a step back and clutch the tampons to my chest. "Do you know Ford Monroe?"

I should've known. Ford Monroe. Panty-dropper extraordinaire. Master of climaxes and killer of relationships before they start.

Yes, I know Ford. Really well. "He's my partner."

And I don't want to hear about his magical tongue. But I'm going to give him shit about it, and I can't wait.

She grins and I know what's coming next. How rude would it be to run? It's bad enough that I don't have any girlfriends of my own, friendships that weren't orchestrated because of our last names and what we could do for each other's careers, but I don't want to attract fake friends who only want to scale me to reach my partner.

"Oh." She oozes excitement. "Can you pass him a message for me?"

The thing about Ford is that he's also my closest friend. I read between the lines. "Didn't he give his number to you?"

She pouts. "I'm sure he hit a wrong number."

He didn't hit any numbers. I know Ford. He's a good guy, but he breaks hearts and expectations because he refuses to make any promises he's not willing to keep. It's why we work so well together. He's hung up on his ex and my last relationship was over as soon as my fiancé dipped his dick back into *his* ex.

Ford and his insanely good looks were off-limits the moment I heard his sob story from one of the EMTs we work with. And since we work together, he knows he can't hit it and quit it with me.

It's a win-win.

"Maybe you could just give me his digits and I'll text him?" she asks hopefully. Her friend rolls her eyes.

I'm right there with you.

"Sorry, I can't give it out. HIPAA and all that." HIPAA's confidentiality requirements have nothing to do with it. Here's hoping these two aren't in the medical field and won't call me on my bullshit.

"Oh, right. Can you tell him Courtney said he can hit her up anytime? I sent him my contact info."

I doubt it. He deletes numbers if he thinks they're going to want more, whether it's breakfast the next morning or a springtime wedding.

But as much as I like Ford and respect the hell out of him as a paramedic, I can't let this poor thing wait on a message that isn't coming.

"I can, but I've got to be honest. He's the definition of commitment-phobe and he probably won't reach out."

Her expression falters. "Oh. I thought we had a connection."

"He's like that, but I can tell you that, truly, it's not you; it's him."

She cocks her head, her gaze sharp. "Are you two together?"

I snort. "No."

Not only is the idea of dating Ford ludicrous—I mean, we're partners—but I'm so not his type. I wear my hair in a plain braid every day to work. I use a sports bra to cram the ladies down because I refuse to do what my mom calls the Baywatch Bounce walking up to a scene. And I don't wear a lick of makeup. Stroke patients don't care if I have mascara on or not. After the way I grew up, it's freeing and I love it.

"Really? Like, never? You're gorgeous."

I relax. She's not going to shoot the messenger, and I'll take a compliment from a woman any day over a dude. She wants in Ford's pants, not mine. "Thanks, but I have my own baggage. It's why we work so well together." I give a smile before glancing at my watch. "Oh, crap, I gotta go."

I rush through checkout and fly to the ambulance garage. Ford's in a huddle with the two guys on the outgoing shift of the ambulance we're assigned to.

Ford lifts his vivid blue gaze from the conversation and grins. "Wescott. You're late."

I give him a mock glare. I'm five minutes early and he knows it. It's just not as early as I usually am.

I swagger toward the group and hit them all where it hurts. A woman's period. "I had to stop for some lady plugs. You want to do it for me next time?"

His brows pop. "You're a lady?"

Mitch's grunt shakes his fledgling gut. He jokes about putting on the pounds with his wife while they were expecting their second kid—who's ten now—but the paramedic could still haul a stair chair down eight flights on his own if he was allowed to.

His partner, Arnesh, an EMT like me, clears his throat and looks around the plain garage bay like he wishes he was anywhere else but here, discussing the periods of someone he knows. He's a rookie like me, but I'm a few years older.

"Relax, Arnesh. Ford here is insecure because I have bigger muscles than him."

Ford scoffs. "In your mouth, maybe."

Mitch's eyes go wide, no doubt worried about a harassment charge based on proximity.

Ford throws his hands up. "Totally not what I meant."

I laugh and pat his shockingly hard shoulder. "I know, and you'd never know anyway." Since Arnesh pales like he's going to faint, I spin the conversation back around to work. "Anything new?"

"Nah," Mitch answers. "It's been a pretty mellow day. But now people are gearing up for Saturday night stupid. It's going to be busy."

The guy has a sixth sense when it comes to the chaos level of the workday. If he says it's going to be busy, it usually is.

"But nothing like next week will be," Arnesh interjects and gives us an ominous stare. "It's a full moon."

We all groan, but then Ford and I share a triumphant look. The last full moon that landed on a weekend was one of the most memorable of my career. Three seizure calls, a guy wandering the street buck naked and bleeding from his nose with a blood alcohol limit over point three, and a five-car pileup on the interstate that had us working until nearly our next scheduled shift.

Ford and I are off next weekend.

Mitch catches the exchange. "Aw, you fuckers. You're not working? Want some extra hours?"

"I have to do my nails," I deadpan. I don't wear polish, and I don't care what length I'm allowed on the job; they're always trimmed short. Not suffering another manicure is one of the perks of moving away from San Francisco. I might still polish my toenails, but these guys will never see me outside of my Under Armour boots.

Ford grins. "I have a date."

"Yeah," Mitch rumbles. "When don't you have a date?" He juts his chin up at Arnesh and they head to the break area, where they'll grab their belongings and leave.

I start for the rig. "Speaking of dates, I ran across one of yours in the store. I gave her your phone number." When color leaches from his face, I can't help chortling. I don't let him suffer long. "Just kidding. I told her not to get her hopes up."

"You're the best."

"As long as you remember that." I stop with my foot on the first step into the patient compartment. "But what is that thing you do with your tongue that she was gushing about?"

His brows draw together. "Give them an orgasm?"

"Oh, so that's why they all chase after you? There's a serious lack of female orgasm-giving males in the world?" My own life has a serious lack of orgasms, thanks to my cheating ex. Whenever I try to get myself off, I hear the moans coming from my ex's office last year.

"Apparently. It's not like I'm a catch."

I roll my eyes, but he doesn't see me. That's his ex talking. "Don't spout her poison, Ford."

That he opened up to me about his ex and how she raked him over velvet-covered coals still surprises me, but I don't take his trust for granted.

I start our equipment check. Mitch and Arnesh never fail to restock the ambulance, but we always check when we start our shift. Even if it weren't policy, we'd do it anyway. There's nothing worse than being on a call and opening a compartment or a bag to find the supplies we need are missing. Not only is it potentially dangerous for the patient, it's embarrassing as hell, and the firefighter first responders on the scene have a long memory.

At every emergency service grill out, I still hear *Hey, Wescott. Got a Band-Aid?*

I had a pediatric case. Unlike Ford, I suck with kids, but this little guy loved Band-Aids. He had a high fever and while Ford got his IV in, I distracted him with bandages. Then later that shift, a fireman cut his finger and asked for one.

I couldn't find a single one and they've never let me forget it. An ambulance with no Band-Aids? Riots of laughter.

With our precheck done inside, we do a walk-around before Ford climbs behind the wheel. He always drives first. I had a few partners during training, and some never failed to point out how they're the paramedic and I'm the EMT, and not just any EMT, but the basic level that can't insert IVs or intubate. Some wouldn't let me do much more than drive. But not Ford. For a player, he has surprisingly little ego.

My phone buzzes as soon as I shut the door. Since we're still in the bay, I sneak a peek. Dread sweeps through me at the name on the screen.

I stare at it, letting it ring.

Ford shamelessly leans over to look. He lets out a long whistle. "What the hell does he want?"

"It's still campaign season," I mumble. My ex is running for California state senator. A big step in his political climb. "And he wants my mother's backing. He probably thinks he can sweet-talk me back." Samuel never quit trying to reconcile. It's hard not to fall for his sincerity. He already has my mother's support—more than I do.

"Answer it and tell him to fuck off."

My mind hangs on the *answer it* part and I hit the green button. Panic seizes my lungs. *Oh, shit. Now what?* "Hello?"

I stare at Ford, horrified that I went so far. He mouths, *whatever it is, no.*

"Aurelia," Samuel croons in that smooth-as-French-silk-pie voice I used to crave hearing, and dammit, I still do. Ford has his baggage. Samuel is mine. "I wasn't sure you'd pick up."

I quit telling him years ago to call me Lia like everyone else. *I'm not everyone else and neither are you.* The guy flings platitudes like parade candy. "I'm just starting my shift. What do you need?"

A bite of smugness fills me at the mention of my job. Being an EMT is a far cry from my UCLA political science degree. Samuel blames himself for the sudden change in my career, but it was the best decision I ever made and I made it for me alone.

"I'll be near Fargo tomorrow and thought I could swing by. We can do lunch."

The panic roars back. *He'll be in Fargo?* "Uh—How are you going to be near Fargo?" Samuel lives in San Francisco.

"Senator Rodriguez, you remember him? He's at some training in Minneapolis and wanted me to attend with him. Anyway, I just want to talk."

There's that soft tone, the one that reminds me of how storybook romantic he could be and just how special I felt when we were together. Up until I wasn't. "Samuel."

"Please, Aurelia."

The genuine remorse in his voice gets to me. He fucked up and he knows it. He regrets it. It would've been one thing if I'd just been a rung on the ladder climb of his career. But we'd been in love, only I'd loved him more. It took me walking away to show him how much he loved *me* and not just my political connections.

I wish falling out of love were as easy as falling in love.

"Just lunch." Beside me, Ford is shaking his head and I avoid eye contact. I have to be strong in the ways I know how. I can't keep running from Samuel forever. "Where?"

"I saw that Fargo has a country club. Let's eat there. Eleven?"

"I'll meet you there." Samuel doesn't know where I live, meaning my parents have respected my wishes and kept it private despite how much they were looking forward to having Samuel as a son-in-law. If he knew my address, I have no doubt I'd be getting floral bouquets that would make the queen of England proud. Or worse—he'd show up on my doorstep. He's too smooth, too repentant, for me to last long against that.

Why did I agree to lunch again? As I disconnect, I avoid Ford's stare.

"I thought you didn't want him back." There's a teasing note in his voice, but there's curiosity, too.

"It's only lunch," I mutter. Scowling, I buckle my seat belt. "Besides, I can't hide from him forever. I can be a big girl and stick to my decision."

"Promise me you'll pour a glass of water on his crotch."

My lips twitch. "I already did that."

"Ice water?"

I nod.

"Good girl. Every time you want to fall under his 'but baby, you mean so much to me' spell, picture the look on his face when you did that."

Samuel's too suave to use a corny line, but Ford's onto something. I can't forget my ex's face when I asked him what had happened in his office with Olivia. Precise denial turned into abject regret when I told him I'd heard everything and caught a glimpse of even more. He'd nearly broken down in front of me, dropping to his knees to beg me to hear him out.

But he was too busy brushing ice off his crotch by that point and I was walking out of the restaurant, deciding what I really wanted to be when I grew up. Attending to his political campaign, or anyone else's for that matter, no longer held any appeal.

"I'm lunching on Saturday, too," Ford says.

I glance at his strong profile. Even after a year of being his partner, I can't believe he's real. A brooding chin straight out of a Jane Austen movie. A hard body carved from granite. A nose with a slight tilt from a break when he was a teenaged lifeguard and got headbutted by a kid he was helping out of the pool. Dirty-blond hair that looks as good messy as it does perfectly combed.

If Samuel had Ford's level of good looks, I would've been toast.

"Your mom?" That's the only lady Ford lunches with.

"Yep."

"Maybe we should switch lunch dates."

"No offense, Wescott, but the way you talk about Samuel, I'm afraid *I'll* succumb to his charms."

I laugh, mostly because he's right. I do go on about Samuel. He was such a big part of my life for so long and it all went south so stereotypically. "Fine. I'll go with my lunch date and wish I were at yours."

"Mom probably wishes you were at mine, too."

Maggie Monroe is a gem, and I can see why Ford did what he did to help her. It wasn't just because he's so driven to prove he isn't like his bio dad. That jackass stepfather of his was a piece of work too, leaving Maggie in such a bind when he died. She only has Ford to help her. It wasn't like her stepchildren were going to lift a finger for her.

The radio comes to life. "Fifty-year-old male in cardiac arrest." As the dispatcher rattles off the address and more details, I flip the lights and sirens on, glad to have something else to focus on.

Because work keeps me from remembering everything I walked away from and how much Samuel and my family are trying to pull me back.

Two

Ford

Is it possible to roll my eyes so hard they clink in the back of my head?

I scowl at one of the city's finest firefighters as he shamelessly flirts with my partner. He'd be a good guy, and he'd be good for her, certainly better than the piece of crap that broke her heart, but does he have to try to pick her up at work?

"Jimmy, you got what you came here for?" I doubt Lia even suspects that Jimmy is being anything more than friendly. She's oblivious to the looks the single firemen throw her way or each other when she walks by. She's striking. I'll give them that. I'm a little over six feet tall and she's only a few inches shorter than me, with a defined frame that's clear even under her unisex polo shirt and boxy pants. I don't think I've ever seen her wear an ounce of makeup, but she doesn't need it. The dazzling amber of her eyes would put any jewelry she wore to shame. Despite the fact that I've only ever seen her in a braid, it doesn't detract from the allure she can't help but give off.

I'd have to be dead not to notice Lia's looks.

As my partner, it doesn't matter. As my friend, I go out of my way not to notice. I don't have many friends, mostly buddies from work. I hang out with some of the firefighters once in a while too. But most of the friends I made in college and medical school are balls deep in their residency. Talking to them only reminds me of where I should be at this stage of my career. That would've been me if I hadn't hit a pileup on the road of life.

Jimmy's expression turns incredulous and he puts his hand to his chest in faux offense. "Am I bothering you, Monroe?" A smirk tilts his lips and his eyes gleam. He thinks I'm being territorial over Lia. I'm not. I'm being protective. She doesn't need to be hit on at work. We've had long talks about how earning respect in her own right is important to her. A firefighter doesn't need to fuck that up.

"You're always a pain in the ass, but Wescott and I have some stocking up to do unless you want to go fetch another obstetrical kit."

Jimmy waves me off and adjusts the suspenders of his uniform. He's a big guy and probably doesn't need to put in as much effort picking up a girl as he is with Lia. "Fine, fine. My shift is over anyway. Let me initial the inspection and let your boss know that the building passed one more time."

I can't keep my scowl away. Every time there's some sort of inspection to do with the building, some young, single fireman shows up when Lia is working, and that means I'm always here to witness the show.

Lia wanders to the supply closet to gather the items we used up during the last two medical calls: a seizure and a broken hip. Jimmy flicks his suspenders and meanders next to me. "Looking a bit green there under the collar, Monroe."

"What the hell are you talking about?" Normally, Jimmy and I get along well. Today, he's a giant pain in the ass. "I'm not sick."

"I'm not talking about you being ill. I think you're jealous." He sings the last word. "If you want to go out with her, you should just ask her. Then me and the guys will start leaving her alone."

"I'm not interested in dating Lia. Maybe you should think about leaving her alone when you're on duty."

"Come on, man. You can't blame us. It's not like she goes to the bars or hangs out with the guys after her shift. The only time we get a chance is when we come here to check your fire extinguishers."

"Did you ever think that she's making sure she doesn't give you assholes the wrong impression?"

Jimmy cocked his head, his gaze appraising. "You're not into her?"

"She's my *partner*." I say it like he should understand the magnitude of that statement, and he should. The people we work with are often more than friends. *Partner* carries a heavy meaning with it. Lia and I save lives together. I don't take that lightly.

"Then I hate to tell you, Monroe, but if you're not going to ask her out, you can't cockblock every other guy from doing it."

The hell I can't. I shake off that thought. I have no business interfering in Lia's dating life, and I'm absolutely not interested in dating her. Risking my job to get laid is not an option, no matter how beautiful and genuine she is. My mom needs the financial help and I need to prove to Cass that I'm not a total fuckup so I can see my son.

I turn away from Jimmy as he walks out and am greeted

by Lia's ass. She's bending over outside the back of the rig, stooping to pick up a sixteen-gauge IV needle packet she must have dropped. I yank my gaze down to the packet on the floor before I can notice how nicely her form fills out her pants. The corner of my mouth curves up. When she nears the ground, she kicks out her left leg like a kickstand. It was one of the first things I noticed about her, and it was what cut the tension between us.

Lia's first impression is regal. The haughty tilt to her nose and her cool demeanor scares many men off, but the reserved way she holds herself is what really makes her stand out. Her tone is firm, but her voice is soft and she always thinks before she acts. My first impression of her is what I've heard called "good breeding." In short, when she was introduced as my new partner, my first thought was that she was too good for me. Then she bent to grab a pen off the floor and kicked a leg out like a giraffe drinking from a flood pool, blowing apart the entitled princess image.

I'm in danger of lifting my gaze to her ass, so instead, I tease her like I'm ten and on the playground again. "Butterfingers."

She straightens with a chuckle, "As always," and climbs into the patient compartment.

I crowd in behind her. "Or did you think Jimmy was still around and you wanted to flash him?"

"Oh my God, you did not just go there."

"Go where?" I ask innocently. "We both know he's been getting bolder. Was that a door he opened for you the other night?"

"He was just being nice—and it was for both of us as we wheeled that pediatric patient out."

A three-year-old I made clown faces at to keep her from crying after a seizure while Lia took her vitals. "I told him to back off."

She stops with a cabinet open and raises a brow. "You did what?"

"He was hitting on you at work. I told him to be professional."

She thinks about it for a moment and shrugs. "Thanks. I don't really want to date right now."

"Got yer back, partner," I drawl.

By the time we finish stocking, the shift is over. I wait for Lia to grab her things so we can walk out together.

"I'm thinking of asking Cass if I can have Jayden for the weekend."

"Think she'll let you this time?"

I wince at the *this time*. But that's how it is. I ask. Cass turns me down. For over two years, I've had to beg and plead for time with my son. Cass's family has money and I don't. She has all the power; she made sure of it, and I can't fight her.

When I can't sleep at night, I dream of suing her ass off for custody.

"I have no idea, but if I ask for a weekend, maybe she'll give me a few hours." Maybe I can overlap that time with going out to eat with my mom. Cass blames her for my fall from future doctor grace and hardly ever lets Jayden around her.

Lia grins. "Playing her. I like it. See you on Wednesday."

"See you." She goes to her car and I go to mine.

The car seat in the back cements my resolve. I call Cass.

"Yeah?" She always sounds irritated when she answers.

"Hey. I have the weekend off. Do you mind if Jayden hangs with me? We can do an overnight."

"The *whole* weekend? Ford, he hasn't been away from home for more than a night."

Which means his other grandparents have had him spend the night. I tamp down the irritation. Letting it out will only make things go in reverse with Cass. "How about just a night?"

"We're going out of town this weekend. Dad's taking us to the Mall of America."

My heart sinks. I can't compete with the Mall of America. "Are you sure you don't want to let him stay here so you can have some adult time?"

"That's just the thing, Ford. I can have adult time and keep it away from Jayden. I can't have him seeing the tramps you trot in and out of your place."

I grind my teeth together. My personal life is none of her business, but she uses it against me whenever possible. I have no rebuttal. Guilty as charged. Going home with a new girl every night off is a lot better than looking at my four walls, wishing I could get to know my son.

"What can I do, Cass? How can I prove that I'm a decent father so you'll trust me with him?"

"Um, maybe start with going on more than one date with someone? The fact that you have to ask is an issue. Christ, Ford. Our son needs a father who can commit to something. Prove you can be a good role model for your son."

She hangs up.

"*Fuck*." I fist my hands and spin around before I do something stupid like hit the frame of my car. I gotta keep my job and breaking my hand would make it hard to do that.

It's not like I dropped out of high school and fucked off with my life. I finished medical school but left medicine before I started my prestigious residency. Mom needed me more.

I might not be a doctor, but I'm out there busting ass every shift to help people. I *am* a good role model. But maybe I have too much of my own dad in me to be a good father.

Three

Ford

"I need you to come to Karoline's wedding with me next weekend."

The sounds of silverware tinkling against plates fade as Mom drops that little bomb on me. Going to my stepsister's wedding is akin to shaving my entire body with a dull razor and then dousing myself in cheap aftershave. "Do we have to go at all?"

"They're making an effort."

I can't believe Karoline invited us in the first place. It's probably her brother Ryan's doing. The peacekeeper. He acts all altruistic as if it's so easy to forget how they treated me and Mom.

I get that they were just kids and didn't see their dad's pattern of treating women like they were interchangeable. Karoline and Ryan were too busy hating on me, their new stepbrother, to pay attention to how abysmally their dad treated me. When he started traveling for "work" and messing around on Mom, she let him. Life was more peaceful when he was gone.

Before Karoline and Ryan's dad, my dad ran out on her when she was pregnant with me. He left her barely out of school with a baby to raise and parents with no interest in supporting her. To this day, I assume she figured staying married to my cheating asshole of a stepfather was better for all of us. Karoline and Ryan wouldn't have to demean another stepmom, and at least this guy would bring home a paycheck.

She paid for that decision. Literally and figuratively. With my help, she's almost paid it all off.

"Do you think you'll bring a date?" Mom asks, hopefulness lacing her tone.

Back to the wedding, I don't want to go. I haven't wanted to go to anything less.

Karoline and her soon-to-be husband, Sergei. Ryan and his wife and kid. Happy. Untouched by their father's bad decisions, while I gave up my career and then my chance at a happy family because of the guy.

No. I can't think of it like that, or the resentment will take over. I did it for Mom. I gave up my dreams of being a doctor for Mom. She needed my help and she had no one—again. Cass gave up on me, on us, and I can't control her decisions.

Cass wanted the perfect life and when she realized she was pregnant, both of us assumed marriage came next. Cass pictured marriage and a baby and me making a healthy six figures. I blew that up when I moved us to Fargo before Jayden was born.

If we couldn't withstand the test of moving here before Jayden was born, then a marriage wouldn't have lasted long anyway. Cass felt like she wasn't a priority and I thought my life partner should still accept me when I turned down having fancy initials behind my name.

I didn't uproot myself, beg for her back, and move to LA to finish my residency, and it cost me my name on Jayden's birth certificate.

I'm going to be alone raising this baby. Why shouldn't my name be the only one on it?

"I'll see what I can do," I say noncommittally, unable to disappoint her. Mom's still rooting for me, thinking I can find a girl, settle down, have babies.

I tried. The girl's tampering with my ability to be a dad. She relegated me to nothing more than a sperm donor, no better than the one who left Mom when two lines appeared on the pregnancy test. So I'm really careful now, to the extent some would call me a manwhore, but that's all right. I don't have to stay home thinking about how amazing it all could've been and my date doesn't get her hopes up that we could be more.

Going to a wedding would definitely get my date's hopes up. Maybe I can find someone and talk to her first. The wedding would be a one-and-done deal. There's gotta be a commitment-phobe lady out there for me, someone who gets not letting down a hardworking mom who takes too much responsibility for my single status.

I scan the restaurant—the *country club*. Mom's new boss gave her a gift card here, an appreciation bonus for her first year on the job. The restaurant portion of the club isn't exclusive to members, but it's as posh as the rest of the place, meant to persuade those on the fence into joining.

My gaze catches on a couple seated on the other side of the dining room. The guy's facing me, a typical good-looking dude in a suit, maybe a few years older than me. His date's back is to me—and what a back it is.

Most guys get hung up on tits or ass, and I've totally

done that too, but with this woman sitting in a chair, I can't see either. Yet her shoulders are bared by the dark-red dress she's wearing. Sleek muscles flex along her back and arms. The back of the dress has a cutout, but her fall of rich mahogany hair covers most of it. *Is her hair as soft as it looks?*

"How's Jayden?" Mom's question is enough to stop me from lusting after the back of a complete stranger.

I force myself to remain relaxed. Mom's sensitive about my issues with Cass. She thinks she's to blame, and Cass would probably agree, but it's only been Cass limiting my time with Jayden. "He's good. I guess Cass and her family are at the Mall of America this weekend."

"Oh, that'll be a nice trip. Will you be seeing him soon?"

The conversation from the other day crashes down on me. Will I be seeing my son soon? Isn't that what I ask myself every day? Cass allows me just enough time with Jayden to give me hope while showing me she's the one with all the power.

I missed his first steps. I missed his first words. And each time I do get to see him, he has to get over "stranger danger" before he quits crying. He doesn't know his own father. If Cass gets into a serious relationship, the guy she's with will have a better chance at being Dad than me.

Fears I've been trying to suppress since Cass left me well up. Mom will know something's wrong and think it's something she did. Because my ass of a stepfather always made her think that.

I need a moment, just a chance to process that damn wedding and my future with my kid so I can have a nice lunch with my mom.

"Uh, I don't know. Excuse me, I want to go to the bathroom before we order." I lurch from the table without waiting for a reply. I give myself a mental shake as Cass's words replay in my head.

Prove you can be a good role model for your son.

I can do it. I can quit sleeping around. Suffer shower masturbation for the next however many years. But I can't go back to being a doctor. Mom needs me. She needs me here, and I need an income.

Medical school left me with a lot of debt that paramedic wages weren't ready to pay off. I need to keep working. It just won't be as the doctor that Cass and her surgeon-family want. No residency program is going to want me after taking this long of a break after medical school.

My adviser's warning echoes in my head. *Take a year off, but if you don't get right back in the game, the game isn't going to want you—because this isn't a game. Students at the top of their class are going to be competing for the same slots as you. And they won't have to explain that they couldn't handle life before becoming a doctor.*

He was right *about everything.*

I'll do whatever it takes to be with my kid, even if that means staying in Fargo and being a paramedic until my body breaks down. Then, I'll teach with the EMS program my company offers.

I weave through the tables, heading for the hallway that promises peace on the other side. I'm not so in my head that I don't try to get a glimpse of the beauty with the nice shoulders. But she's gone. Just the guy remains in all his pretentious asshole glory. Not that I know a thing about him other than the arrogant tilt to his lips as he scrolls through his phone.

Looking for her is diversion enough. I'm feeling somewhat better as I hit the hall to the restroom. Then the finest ass appears in front of me, covered in soft burgundy material, swaying gently with each step.

Damn. There she is.

Legs for miles. The full view of her back from the top of

her head all the way to her slender ankles in sharp heels is more amazing than I could've hoped for. The shoes add to her already considerable height, and even that's satisfying. No breaking my back just to steal a kiss.

She lifts a hand to push the ladies' room door open. A clutch drops from under her other arm. The soft curse she utters is vaguely familiar, but I'm stuck on a cloud of anticipation. She's bending to grab it.

I don't have time to be chivalrous and get it for her. That's what I tell myself. Because the show is going to be spectacular.

My steps slow. I don't want to bump around her while she's bent over. Also, a good excuse to keep leering like a perv.

As she reaches the lowest point of her descent, she kicks her left foot to the side.

Air gusts out of my mouth.

"*Wescott?*"

∩∩

Lia

My fingers curl around my clutch and I whip around. "Ford?"

Of all the coincidences, of all the witnesses to my own personal embarrassment and the way I can't seem to stop catering to Samuel O'Hara.

Ford's expression is not one I've seen before and I thought I knew him pretty well. His face is screwed up, equal parts incredulous and horrified. He rears back when I turn around, his gaze drifting down my dug-out-of-storage cocktail dress, confusion clouding out his other emotions.

"What?" My cheeks are burning. "Surprised I clean up well?"

"Wescott?" he repeats. He looks at me like he can't believe my voice is coming out of this body.

My EMT uniform must make me boxier than I thought. "Present and accounted for." I tighten my grip on my clutch. If the damn thing hadn't dropped, I would be safely locked away in the ladies' room, away from Samuel. I just want two minutes to be weak instead of the strong woman I moved to North Dakota to be.

Ford's expression is steeped in disbelief, but I guess he got a faceful of my ass. "I didn't see you here."

He falls back into stunned silence and I don't know what else to do. When his gaze drifts down to my dress, I do a little curtsy. "Didn't recognize me?"

He closes his eyes, shaking his head. When he opens them, he's back to devil-may-care Ford. "Not until your giraffe move."

"My what?"

"When you bend over, you kick a foot out."

I do? Since we're back to being Ford and Wescott, I lean against the wall by the bathroom door, happy to take longer than expected. Samuel's getting under my skin and I had to give myself space. Seeing Ford helps me remember I'm Lia, a competent paramedic, and that I worked hard for that title.

He waves his hand up and down. "I almost didn't recognize you without your dude clothes."

I whack him with my clutch. "They are not dude clothes. They're comfortable and what a lot of women actually wear when they're not out trying to get laid."

His grin is slow, a gotcha gleam in his eyes. "Wescott, are you telling me that you dressed up like this hoping to get laid?"

I suck in a breath.

He grins, his eyes twinkling, but he leans closer like he's hanging on the answer.

"I wanted to show him what he's missing," I hiss.

His grin fades. "You shouldn't have to show him. It should be easy to see exactly how badly he fucked up."

My lips part. He's so earnest and I'm floored. I never thought of it that way. And the way it makes me feel sends up a red flag. Warm flutters in my belly aren't supposed to happen around Ford. "So...meal with your mom going okay?"

His lips thin. "It's good. It's...fine." Before I can ask what's really going on, he continues, "You?"

"Same." I sigh and rest my head on the cool wall. "It's fine, but the message is clear. He wants me back. We were good together. We worked so well. Of course, my parents love him..."

Ford's forehead crinkles. "But he dipped his wick in some other woman's candle."

"Coated it good from what I could hear. Anyway, he can try all he wants." I hug my arms around myself, grateful to have escaped Samuel's orbit for a few minutes. It's too hard not to be drawn in.

Proving that he knows me better than anyone, Ford says, "You don't have to see him again. It doesn't matter what your parents want."

I nod, dropping my gaze from his dark-blue eyes. My parents. More my mother. She adores Samuel. He reminds her of herself, and his indiscretion is only a blip on the radar as far as she's concerned. *A mistake he won't make again, she insisted.* "She messaged me before I got here. Told me to tell her how it went."

"And 'we had drinks and caught up and went our separate ways' won't cut it?"

Wouldn't that be easy? "I wish I could actually enjoy being around my mother again."

He lifts a shoulder. "You could tell her you're dating again."

"But then I'd have to pony up an actual person for her inspection, and I don't have the energy to invest in a guy for even a pretend date."

"Same," he says, surprising me.

"Your mom wants you to get together with Cass again?"

"No. It's more Cass who's putting pressure on me to get into a stable relationship. As if she didn't shatter all my expectations of how one's supposed to go."

It's nothing but a power trip for Cass. The only child of prominent doctors, she couldn't stand that Ford chose his mother over her, and her caustic remarks left scars. He won't settle down until he meets someone who can undo all the damage she did.

I smile wryly. "So we both need a significant other to show everyone that we're just fine on our own."

He peers at me, his mind working behind his sharp blue eyes. His gaze narrows and then widens, a slow grin spreading across his lips. "What if we—" He shakes his head.

"What?"

He doesn't get a chance to finish.

"Aurelia?"

My stomach sinks. Samuel has come looking for me. It's what he does. Makes me feel special. Like I'm the center of his world, like I mean something to him.

I've been trying so hard to forget him, and I thought I could do this meal without old feelings smothering the hurt he caused, but it's backfiring. Just looking at Samuel makes it hard to forget the good times. A suit tailored to his body like a second skin. His hair parted down the side like he walked straight out of *Mad Men.*

Ford mouths *Aurelia?* and I glare at him. Only my parents and Samuel call me by my full name. But my annoyance turns to bewilderment when he swivels around and snakes his arm around my waist, tucking me into his side. Instead of the cool wall, I'm pressed against a furnace. A hard furnace. Rock hard.

What the hell is he doing?

"You must be Samuel," Ford replies, his tone smooth and extra rich. "Wesco—Lia's told me so much about you."

Either I play along with whatever Ford is doing, or I risk looking like a fool, and Samuel's made me feel foolish too many times. Ford's arm tightens around me, and instead of going rigid and stepping away, I relax into his hold. We've worked closely together for a year, but this is definitely the closest we've ever been. And like working with him, this feels comfortable, but it's growing more uncomfortable for reasons I don't care to inspect. Reasons that have to do with how good he feels and how hot my body is growing.

Samuel's gaze hardens on Ford. My ex might be genuinely remorseful about us, but he also hates losing or looking like a fool. Ford's threatening on both accounts.

"I'm sorry," Samuel says, adjusting his tie. "You are...?"

Ford extends his hand but doesn't let me go. "Ford Monroe. Lia's partner at work, and her boyfriend outside of work."

I manage to school my features before Samuel's gaze jerks to mine. My smile must look more like a rigid grimace. "Ford and I..." I chuckle nervously. "Are dating?"

It sounds more like a question. Are we doing this?

So we both need a significant other to show everyone that we're just fine on our own.

He'll be my boyfriend for the benefit of my mother and Samuel, and I'll be his girlfriend for the benefit of Cass.

We'll pretend to date. No problem.

Except I'm supremely aware of his embrace.

A furrow forms between Samuel's brows. "I didn't realize you, uh, that you were seeing someone."

Ford saves me. "We haven't come out in the open yet since we work together and all. We wanted to prove to everyone that we can do both without it affecting our job." He lifts a shoulder, his arm still around me. He makes me feel petite and not many men can do that. "But I happened to be here with my mom and you caught us, so I guess this is the day we'll announce the big news."

"Congratulations," Samuel says woodenly.

Guilt gnaws at me. For the deception. For making Samuel feel like crap and like an idiot for driving out here from his conference to woo me back. But I'm tired of the pull toward him when he hurt me so badly. All I have to do is remember the ecstatic sounds his ex made while she was bent over the mahogany desk he said always reminded him of the color of my hair. My resolve hardens.

He shoves his hands in his pockets and spears me with his dark, intense gaze. "So you haven't told your parents yet?"

"No. I'll talk to them later. They've been so busy."

His nod is deliberate, but his mouth is pressed in a line. His gaze bores into me like he senses the lie. Ford knows me, but Samuel knows me almost as well, and in ways my partner doesn't.

"I didn't mean to party crash," Ford says. "But since we're all here, you two are welcome to join Mom and me. She doesn't know yet either, but she'll be delighted. She loves Lia."

That part is true at least, but my stomach churns at lying to his sweet mom. She's endured a lifetime of lies.

"No, I should probably get going." Samuel pins me with

his amber stare. "Don't worry about the tab, Aurelia. I'll take care of it."

There he goes, being a good guy again. Taking the high road when he could ream me out for drawing him in and not telling him I was taken, which, in my defense, I didn't know yesterday. "I appreciate it, Samuel. It was nice to see you again."

He gives me a look that asks *Was it?* and I offer a tentative smile. He threw away five years in a second. I wish I could do the same. I'll settle for amicable if only to help myself get over him.

He strides away, but Ford and I don't move, standing alone outside the restrooms.

"I can't believe we're doing this," I mutter.

"You and me both. But it makes sense. Cass can't find any fault with you."

She'll try. "My mother will find so much fault with you because you're not Samuel."

A low rumble leaves his chest and I grin up at him, startled that his face is inches away. Surprise lifts his brows, and he tugs his arm away from me and stuffs his hand in his pocket. "Then I'll have to use my charm more than ever."

"How long are we going to do this?" I have a fake boyfriend and the pressure's been lifted from my chest. I can take a full breath. Samuel's attempts to win me back have been deflected, and I have someone to help battle my parents. But this is Ford. I doubt he does even fake dating for long.

"As long as we need to." He holds his elbow out and I wrap my hand around his arm. "I guess that was our test drive. Ready to see my mother?"

∩∩

Ford

Pretending to be Lia's boyfriend is both my best and my worst idea. Samuel's not giving up on her. He was congenial and he might've conceded today, but I didn't see defeat in his eyes. He's biding his time, and his question about whether or not Lia's parents know said everything. He has Mrs. Wescott's full support and she can wear Lia down better than anyone. It's why Lia's in a different state and not in California.

Mom likes Lia, if only because she's a girl I actually talk about and all in a positive light. I think even Mom knows that if I haven't tried to date Lia, she must be someone special. Cass will find it difficult to use her against me when it comes to Jayden. Unlike me, Lia doesn't sleep around, she wasn't responsible for the breakup of her last long-term relationship, and she comes from a family possibly more affluent than Cass's.

However, if this plan goes balls-up, I'll lose my best friend and a damn good partner.

Lia's hand is loose around my elbow as we walk to the table. Mom looks up and smiles at us both. The server's filling Mom's water and sees me coming.

"Shall I get another place setting?" she asks as she tops off my water next.

"Yes, please." I ask Lia, "Did you already order your food with—" I almost mention Samuel, but Mom's gaze jumps from our faces to Lia's hand on me.

"No. Not yet." She smiles and it cuts right through me like nothing else. This one is a full-on politician's daughter. Her hair shines under the lights and the gloss on her lips only enhances how full they are. She embodies grace and refinement. Take her photo and put her on the cover of *Time*.

That look only raises the stakes higher. This is the Lia that the world got before she climbed into the cab of the ambulance with me. I don't know this Lia, the one that can smile and turn aside invasive questions about her and her parents and say the right things to cement her fiancé's political climb. The Lia I know, Wescott, is real. She no longer has the fiancé and she's the one who bitches about arrogant ER residents who think they're gods to be worshiped by everyone else in the hospital.

"Hi, Mrs. Monroe."

I pull out the chair between mine and Mom's.

"Please, call me Maggie."

Lia takes a seat, sweeping her hands under her to straighten her dress. My blood heats as I make the mistake of looking down. Her waist dips and flares over the generous curves of her hips. Lia has a knockout body, and now I can't pretend not to know.

"Mom, Lia and I wanted to talk to you about something."

Mom's steady gaze settles on me. "Oh?"

"We're dating." I sit and grip my water, the cool condensation wetting my hand, covering the nervous sweat breaking out over my body.

The only other girl I brought home as an adult was Cass, and that was the most uncomfortable two hours of my life. It was like Cass conducted both an interrogation and a financial audit at the same time. Since my stepfather was alive at the time, Mom was oblivious about the true state of her affairs, talking investments and 401(k) plans, both of which were my stepfather's fabrications. He'd spent all the money.

I'd been too enamored with Cass to be embarrassed

until she made a comment afterward. *Good thing you're going to be a doctor. I can't imagine my parents being able to carry on a conversation with yours.*

So many red flags I ignored. Never again.

"Oh?" Mom's expression doesn't change. "Dating? Don't you still work together?"

"Yes, we're still partners," I say. Here I am, getting Mom's hopes up. Just what I didn't want to do, but if I pretend to date Lia and we pretend to end things amicably, maybe Mom will worry less.

Anxiety churns in my gut, yet I hang on to the excuse.

"Natural transition." Lia's smile is serene, and she's poised like she's doing an interview, which this kind of resembles. The server leans over her shoulder to place a glass of ice water in front of her. "Thank you so much."

She takes a long sip like she's on the beach, watching the sunset and not lying to my mother in a classy restaurant. I chug mine like it's cheap beer. Her only tell is the rigid line of her shoulders, but if I wasn't so used to reading her body language from our work together, I wouldn't be able to tell.

Mom looks at me. Really inspects me, like she can detect the lie between us. Then her demeanor relaxes and she smiles. "This lunch is turning out better than I thought. Are you coming to the wedding?"

Four

Ford

I straighten my tie and walk up to Lia's front door. This last week, we've ignored the whole dating ruse and concentrated on work during our shifts, trading only details of times and arrangements for today. Otherwise, I tried not to think about seeing Lia outside of work or how pleasant lunch with Mom had been.

The blinds flutter in the picture window of the condo next door.

"Evening, Mrs. Rosenthal," I call, in case the nosy neighbor is listening in, too.

She peers back out between the gap in her drapes, her owlish eyes leering at me. I still can't tell if she's guarding Lia or just distrustful of me. Probably the former. Mrs. Rosenthal was a friend of Lia's grandma. Lia's told me the stories of growing up, learning to play bridge with Mrs. Rosenthal while sitting on her grandma's lap, and listening to them swap stories about being nurses.

Mrs. Rosenthal jerks back and the curtains ripple shut. I repress a smile and knock on the plain brown door. Unlike Mrs. Rosenthal's place, there's no garish wreath smothering the plank of wood, no gnome's ass sticking out of the flower bed. There's little more than weeds on Lia's side of the flower bed. Her place is as unadorned as she is.

Good thing her mother hasn't been here yet. She's all about appearances, and I doubt this condo would pass what Lia calls her press test. *Will it look good in the press?*

Lia said her grandma used to joke that she would never plant flowers. That way, Elaine Wescott would never bring the media circus to her doorstep. Is that what Lia's doing?

Before I can knock, the door swings open. Lia's in another dress, one the color of sunshine hidden behind thin clouds, subdued enough that she probably thinks she won't steal attention from the bride. It'll be hard for me to take my eyes off her. The chaste neckline manages to show off her shoulders but covers her cleavage. A shame. The gauzy material swirls just above her knees but doesn't hide how long and defined her legs are.

"Nice," slips out before I can smother the tone full of male appreciation.

Pink infuses her cheeks, but her gaze streaks across my chest. "Thanks. You look, uh, good, too."

"It's not the white polo."

Her expression turns almost shy. "No, it's not, but you look good in that, too."

I stuff a hand in my pocket. I pride myself on being a regimented guy, but my self-discipline is flagging when it comes to keeping my greedy eyes off of the material draping over her breasts and hugging her hips. "Ready?"

"If I say no, does that change anything?"

"It'll be fun. It's only stepsiblings I've never been close to and their mom who detests my mom."

"What could go wrong?" She tilts her head to the left, the movement so tiny only I would notice. "Is Mrs. Rosenthal spying on us?"

"Do Arnesh's hands still shake during an IV start?"

Her lips quirk and my attention hooks on them. She's wearing lip gloss. Is it the high-end kind that tastes like sanitizer? Or the berry-flavored cheap stuff that would make her lips even more lickable than they already are? "She was telling me yesterday that she has a grandson who's never had a serious girlfriend and we'd get along great."

I shoot Mrs. Rosenthal's condo a hard look. Her grandson had better live across the country and be afraid of flying. He doesn't need to come anywhere near Fargo. Lia starts down the walk and I jog a few steps to keep up. "And you told her you're taken?"

"She's been trying to set me up with him since I was fifteen." She pauses and turns back. "But how far are we taking this?"

"It has to be believable."

"Believable enough that I have to lie to everyone around me?"

We're both stopped halfway between her front door and the street where I'm parked. "That's kind of how it goes. We don't know who she's talking to." Lia probably does, but my lame excuse is out there.

"She gets her groceries delivered and I think the mice living in her eighties Cadillac will learn to drive it before she ever fires up the engine again."

"Maybe that grandson of hers should fix it for her," I joke, but crankiness has set in since hearing she's known this mysterious single guy for ten years.

She gives me a funny look and keeps walking.

I let out a quiet breath. I might've overreacted, but I have more to lose than she does. "Look, if Cass catches wind that we're pretending, she'll never leave Jayden with me again." I don't make enough to fight a long legal battle and her parents will throw everything they have behind it.

"I get it, Ford." She stops at the passenger door and I automatically open it for her. She lifts a dark brow, her gaze jumping between the door and me.

"I have manners, Wescott."

"I never said you didn't. Don't start opening the ambulance door for me." Getting in, she arranges her dress. "All right. According to everyone from here on out, I'm taken."

"Thank you." I mean it. She's no longer just a sounding board about Cass's unfairness. Now, she's my lifeline, a way to show the world that I'm stable father material.

I close the door and jog around to the other side. The drive to the wedding venue is quiet. As I pull into the lot, I spot Mom's car. She's sitting inside as if she can't bring herself to go in alone. I'm glad I agreed to come. Even more grateful to Lia. Between the both of us, this might be a nice day for Mom.

I park as close as I can and lead Lia to Mom. When I knock on the window, Mom jumps, her guilty gaze flicking to the window. She opens the door and clambers out.

"Oh," she says, adjusting her own floral dress and smoothing it down. "I was just, uh... I was waiting for you."

"Safety in numbers?" I mutter, and she scowls, but it quickly disappears. Lia's hand slips into mine and I give it a squeeze, grateful for the support.

Mom begrudgingly nods. "I'm sure it'll be fine."

"Or they'll ignore us and it'll be painfully awkward."

"Ford Monroe," Mom huffs, but she knows I'm right. Trying not to be assholes when they cross paths at the grocery store is different than not giving Mom the time of day at a big family event. She glances at Lia. "Thank you for coming."

The change in Mom is subtle, but it's there. Pride. A woman of Lia's caliber is here with me, and now Mom can show us off here, among people she's forever failed to impress.

"It's my pleasure," Lia says warmly. "What's dating if there aren't awkward wedding dances involved?"

Mom's laugh surprises her as much as me and she starts for the door of the venue, her feet lighter than a minute ago. I give Lia a grateful smile and ignore the spark in my chest. Cass would've said something vaguely insulting and bitched to me about the wedding all night if she even talked to me again the rest of the night.

It's quiet in the event center, but an usher waits for us and leads us through to the courtyard behind the building. The sun is out with a few fluffy clouds in the sky as if one of the guests ordered perfect weather for an outdoor wedding as a gift to the bride and groom. A white canopy stretches over several rows of chairs with an elegant floral archway on one end. People I don't recognize mill around, all dressed similarly to me in my casual blue suit and Lia in her soft dress.

Mom's steps falter when she sees the mother of the bride flitting around the crowd, happier than a hummingbird guzzling nectar. Lia and I fall in step next to her, pillars of support. During her marriage, Mom was vilified by my stepsiblings. All they knew was that their dad had left their mom and moved on to another woman. All they saw was me living with him full time while they only got him part of the time. They didn't know he ignored me most of my life— if I was lucky. The unlucky times, he needled and picked at all my insecurities. He was good at that.

After my stepdad's secrets were exposed, she was humiliated. I only know a portion of her pain. I should've seen it coming. I should've known that his business trips were nothing more than stereotypical write-offs with other women.

My stepbrother breaks away from the group. Several years older than me, his eyes crinkle as he greets Mom. His smile seems genuine, and for once, I see him as a thirty-six-year-old man and not a petulant fifteen-year-old.

"Maggie. How nice to see you." Ryan lifts his gaze to me and extends his hand. "Ford."

"Ryan. This is Lia Wescott."

Ryan shakes my hand, his curious gaze on Lia, full of obvious questions that are more insulting than I care to admit. Did I pick her up last night at some bar and convince her to come today? Is she the type to get drunk and make a scene? There's no way she's as refined as she looks if she's my date.

I answer some of the questions. "Lia and I are also partners on the ambulance. We're dating."

Mild shock registers on his face. "Ah. Lia. That's why your name's so familiar. Maggie's mentioned you a time or two."

She has? I'm not shocked Mom talks about me. But Ryan remembered? I prepare myself for a subtle dig or a not-so-subtle one like what he used to do when we were kids, but nothing comes.

"Nice to meet you," Lia's warm tone puts all of us at ease. "Lovely venue."

Ryan shoves his hands in his pockets. "Yes, well, Karoline has exceptional taste. She takes after our mother that way."

My smile tightens. Ryan might not have meant that as a dig toward Mom, that his dad had shit taste, but I can't help my reaction.

I take Mom's elbow and tug Lia with me at the same time. "We'll find our seats. Thanks, Ryan."

When we're several feet away, Mom mutters, "That went better than I hoped, but I guess I haven't talked to them much in the last few years."

"I still don't trust him."

Mom pats my arm. "He was an angry kid and a bitter young man. Maybe family life has balanced him." She tips her head toward two young girls in twirly white dresses. Girls who could've been nieces had I been allowed to be some sort of brother to Ryan and Karoline.

Lia remains quiet as we take our seats. Thankfully, we don't have to talk to anyone else before the ceremony starts.

Lia crosses one long leg over the other. The movement catches my eye, but my gaze lingers on her satiny skin. She has amazing legs. Shoulders. Hair. What body part am I going to admire next? Fucking toes?

On cue, my gaze trails down to her white strappy sandals and the breath whooshes out of me. Her toenails are bubble-gum pink.

Bubble-gum pink.

Lia Wescott. The woman who never wears jewelry, has never been seen with a manicure, and doesn't use a dab of makeup paints her damn toenails.

Lust rips into me. I clear my throat and tear my gaze away. Lia peers at me from the corner of her eye, no doubt concerned that someone else is approaching to piss me off. I wish that's what had caused my reaction and not my wanting to strip Lia down and find out what other surprises are in store.

She's my *friend*. Is it normal to want to fuck your female friend so bad you can barely breathe through the need?

It takes the whole damn ceremony to calm my body down. It has to be the abstinence. I've been laid too regularly since Cass dumped me. My only other stretch of abstaining was when Cass was pregnant and cut me off, but even then, I didn't have a case of blue balls so bad it strangled me *over bubble-gum pink nails.*

Fuck.

I manage to smile and clap when Karoline flounces down the aisle in a wedding dress that billows out in a circle around her.

Ryan lingers behind to invite everyone to the reception and dance afterward. Lia's arm is back in mine and I fight an internal battle to keep my dick down where it belongs. I refuse to get an erection at my stepsister's wedding.

"Want to leave?" I quietly ask Mom.

Mom shakes her head. "We made it through the ceremony, and the RSVP was more for the dinner. It'd be rude to leave before eating. But then I'm taking off. I'll leave it up to you two what you want to do the rest of the reception. You've done enough already. I'm...enjoying myself."

"Are we going to stay for the dancing?" Lia's eyes are bright. My partner, who is all-business and no play, is actually looking forward to playing. She goes somber. "I mean, if the dinner goes well."

I want to leave now. Our encounter with Ryan wasn't bad. But we still have to face Karoline and her mother. It's Karoline's big day. I can't be a dick to her if she says something insulting. Yet, I'm caught not wanting to disappoint Lia. "If everything's going well, I don't see why we can't stay. It's just dancing."

My body, against hers, shaking and grinding... Just dancing. *Right.*

∩∩

Lia

. . .

Ford has a body cut from stone, and right now, he's moving like a giant slab of granite.

When I glance in the direction he's looking, I see the reason. A matronly woman wearing a mother-of-the-bride dress is cutting through the crowd. Her expression is the same as I'd imagine on revolutionary soldiers marching into battle. Stoic, girded, prepared. Her flinty gaze travels over Maggie Monroe to Ford and skips over me. I guess since I'm with Ford, I mean nothing.

"Maggie," the woman greets in a tone that could ice over a lake. Her neat blond bob is losing ground to silver, but she's owning it. Her shoulders are back and her chin's up, like the chip she carries on her shoulder has long been cemented into place.

Ford's mom keeps her expression pleasant. "Helen, what a beautiful wedding."

Helen's smile solidifies until I think it might crack. The way she greeted Maggie and that she kept her married name when Maggie didn't is telling. Ford was never adopted and as soon as his stepfather was in the ground, Maggie went to the courthouse, proudly claiming *I was born a Monroe and my son is a Monroe.*

I've seen it enough in my parents' social circle. Helen Jenkins was still in love with her husband when they divorced and he married Maggie. It didn't matter that he was a cheat and a grade *A* loser. Her loyalty and love couldn't reform him and perhaps she feared Maggie's could. What does she think now that the truth is out?

"I didn't think you'd make it, given that you and the kids weren't close." Is Helen usually this blunt?

"I wouldn't have missed it." Maggie's a class act. Helen reminds me of a rough version of my own mom, saying whatever she can to put herself on the higher ground, but

Maggie just rolls on like Helen's barbs aren't even there. "It was an honor to be invited."

Helen's light brows rise. "And a surprise."

Perhaps the kids are moving beyond their dad's transgressions faster than Helen is. Helen is probably the reason the kids were so hard on Maggie and Ford.

Chalk it up to the two flutes of cheap champagne, but I can't keep my mouth shut. I grew up in politics. For all my mother's faults, she can smooth over awkward situations. "It's just wonderful that you all can come together for a momentous event like this. It certainly speaks of how well you raised Ryan and Karoline. They seem like lovely people, though I admit, I haven't met the bride yet."

Helen is blinking at me as if I just walked straight out of the hedgerow behind us and barged into the conversation. "Yes, well, they turned out very well. Despite *everything*."

I hope she means everything, as in their father, but the cool way she regards Maggie, I'm not sure. Helen's type needs constant distraction and flattery. "Karoline's dress is gorgeous. What an eye for taste."

Helen's struggle to dismiss me is brief, but she caves under the compliments toward her daughter, her pride and joy. "It's a Carolina Herrera. Her husband insisted she get what she wants."

"He's a very lucky man."

Helen beams. Score. She's about to tell me more. I'm sure to gush about how lucky he really is and how fortunate Karoline is, but someone calls her name. "If you'll excuse me."

Maggie lets out a hard breath, deflating like a Macy's Day balloon. "I can't believe that went well." She touches my arm. "Thank you."

Ford's brows drop and his scrutiny is unnerving. I've told him about this part of my life, but the only part he's seen in action is when I'm trying to convince a patient that they really should go to the hospital. "It's not a problem. I grew up around a bunch of Helens."

Ford's inspection deepens. Did I upset him?

Maggie chuckles. "Well, I can tell you that I'm not used to having such savvy backup. You're officially invited to everything I ever have to do with the Jansens in the future." She gathers her clutch and drains her water. "On that note, I'll give Karoline my regards as I leave, but my nerves can't take more. You two stay and have fun. I have no doubt you'll be fine." Her grin is wry as she looks at Ford. "Just stick close to that one."

She pulls him down for a hug. Watching his big body curl around his petite mom tugs my heartstrings. Everyone else sees his cocky, confident side, the competent paramedic with the easy charm that gets him into women's pants with just a smile. They think everything comes easy to him, but I know better. I see how hard he tries to be a decent person, and his main motivator is Maggie.

When she leaves, we stand by the table, watching the reception workers clear the dance floor and the live band set up.

"Thank you," is all he says.

"Anytime." I glance at him. With the sun setting and sconces glowing, his expression is shadowed, brooding. "Are you okay?"

"Now that the big face-off with Helen was so anticlimactic. I came prepared for veiled insults or constant sniping meant to hurt Mom, but..."

He has a bunch of adrenaline and nowhere to use it.

The first chords of a slow dance drift through the tent. The lead singer calls the bride and groom out. Once their dance is done, a faster song plays.

I yank Ford along with me. This will be the best way to

burn off all his restless energy. "Come on. Show me your moves."

"The only moves I have are horizontal," he growls, his timbre vibrating right through me.

"I've heard. Just pretend it's sex with your clothes on."

The hot look he gives me sears me down to my bones. My heart stutters. This is the Ford I don't let myself see. Until today, I've purposely tried to ignore Ford's sexiness, but there are moments when it's impossible, moments like now. His hair is combed to the side but artfully mussed. His suit jacket is unbuttoned, and the dress shirt below only highlights the expanse of his chest.

I shove the thought away. Ford's hot. I've always known that. Right now, I'm going to concentrate on how excited I am to dance with someone who doesn't make me feel like Godzilla stomping a small city.

My heels put me almost even with him, but he's said nothing. Absolutely nothing. Samuel used to joke that he'd better start taking a calcium supplement to ward off osteoporosis, or I'd surpass him in height. Then there were the jokes that he'd replace all my heels with flats. He said it enough that my height must have really bothered him, maybe not a lot at first, but it's one of those things that got worse as we dated and his insecurities grew.

Not Ford. Like everything else, he's unapologetically secure in his size, and while he's taller than Samuel, he isn't threatened I wear heels that show he's still mortal.

I don't threaten his masculinity and that's a heady feeling, one I haven't experienced since after my growth spurt in eighth grade when I suddenly towered over everyone. Middle school dances were a test of my fortitude and I wore flats all through high school to keep from standing out.

I never wore anything with more than a two-inch heel during my years with Samuel.

On the dance floor, Ford hooks my hand, spinning me into a little twirl. A laugh ripples through me, but the next second, I'm back in his arms, his hand sliding around my waist and pulling me close. I automatically drape one arm around his shoulder and grip his other hand, hoping my skin isn't suddenly clammy.

Because this is nice. His hold is strong. Confident.

"I thought you didn't know how to dance." My accusation comes out breathy and there's probably a telltale flush creeping up my chest.

My partner. He's my *partner*. We are not dating. We're only faking.

But my body refuses to listen and my mind is stuck on the "sex with clothes on" comment I foolishly made.

"I don't care to dance. I didn't say I don't know how."

I drop my tone to mimic his. "'The only moves I have are horizontal.'"

The corners of his mouth curl and his eyes twinkle. "Mom loves to dance and"—he murmurs the next part so no one around us hears—"since my stepdad specialized in disappointing her, he made it a point never to waltz with her."

"You can waltz?" We aren't waltzing now. He's doing a slow side to side that all too often lines up my belly with his and I'm reminded how hard his body really is. I'm struggling not to notice how close we are.

If he happens to break out in a more formal dance step, I was trained in all the basics—waltz, foxtrot, two-step. Hell, I can even line dance the Achy Breaky, anything that might come up at a fundraising function my parents attended. It was one of the skills in my arsenal that made me such a good catch for someone like Samuel.

I knew the life, I was poised, and I could smile and defuse tense situations with semi-empty platitudes.

Ford doesn't care about any of that. He cares that I can compress a chest to the beat of "Staying Alive" and traction splint a femur fracture.

"When the need arises, I can waltz." He's speaking low again, an intimate rumble that sends a shiver down my spine. "But this isn't that type of song."

"No. It's junior high all the way. If the band keeps going this route, I might have to start twerking."

His eyes flare and his pupils dilate. His hold on me tightens for a fraction of a second before he shakes himself. "That's not something I need to see."

The curl of disappointment takes me off guard and I snap, "I wouldn't be doing it for you."

He blinks at my sudden vitriol, but dammit, I hate being reminded how boring men find me.

Good breeding trumps loose morals every time, Aurelia. As if Mom saying that ever helped me through my hormone-ridden years.

Ford dips his head close to my ear, his breath wafting over my skin, pebbling my nipples and making a part of me roar to life that's felt dead for too long. "Now, Lia, if you're not shaking that fine ass for your fake boyfriend, you'd better not be teasing anyone else."

My breath coalesces in my throat, smothering an indignant reply that might save me from rubbing myself all over him. So why his vehement reaction about not wanting to see anything that'll make my ass shake?

A woman with a camera pops up at our side. "Hey, you lovebirds. Give me one for the kiss cam."

Hearing *lovebirds* and *kiss cam* yanks me out of the fog of lust I can't seem to shake.

We stop moving, but Ford doesn't let me go. He echoes, "Kiss cam?"

"Yeah," she answers with the vibrancy of someone

young and getting paid to do what she loves. She flicks one of her two braids over her shoulder. Her green dress is a perfect subdued tone. Not bright enough to be garish but not so dark it's giving funeral vibes. The perfect wedding photographer, blending into the surroundings, all the better to ambush people. "I'm surprising the happy couple with a love-inspired theme to their wedding dance photos. You know, showing the bride and groom how their celebration has inspired others to display their love."

My mind is still reeling over "kiss cam." I can't register what she's saying.

"Don't worry, I'll come by later and get the story of how much the bride and groom mean to you for their wedding dance scrapbook. So..." Her grin widens and she puts the camera to her eye. "Give me a kiss."

The word *kiss* rebounds through my brain like a rubber ball in a circular room. It's not just a kiss. It's kissing Ford. We're pretending to date. Where does that say we have to pretend to kiss? And how the hell can one pretend to kiss? It's like pretending to be pregnant.

With one simple flex of his muscles, I'm plastered to Ford, closer than I thought possible, given we were already dancing.

"Give me one for the camera, babe."

I have only enough time to flash him a scowl before he lowers his head. This is the only time I'll ever curse my height with a guy—he doesn't have far to go. Then his warm lips are on mine and I melt into his embrace.

It's not a tentative touch, but he stops at a light press. Until a whimper escapes me and I'm molding around him. Between his secure hold and the firm, commanding touch of his lips, I'm a goner.

He answers by deepening the kiss. I open for him as my

brain shuts everything off but the pleasure center. My nerves are on fire and they want more of what he's giving.

His tongue sweeps in and I meet him, tasting the sweet champagne and chocolate-covered strawberries he shared with me and his mother. I twine my tongue with his, wanting more of his flavor, more of that hot velvet against me, and more of what Ford can do with that tongue.

And then he did this thing with his tongue—

Even the reminder of exactly who he is and the trail of broken hearts he's left around town isn't enough to make me stop. I'm learning what he can do with that tongue and I'm an avid pupil. I fist my hand in the fabric of his coat.

He gently twists my other hand in his and lowers our arms until he's got me securely in his hold, my arm partially around my back. I'm stuck in this position and I don't want to move.

I'm slowly inching my fingers into his hair and angling my head to take him deeper when the photographer's voice breaks through. "That's good for me. Any more and I'll need to put a warning label on the album."

We break apart to her departing laughter. Ford's gaze slashes across my kiss-swollen lips and we're both panting, his chest rapidly rising and falling against mine, increasing the sensitivity of my puckered nipples.

He loosens his hold, snapping his hands away from me. Since we are bound together so tightly, the action sends me stumbling back a step. He catches my arm but pulls his hand back once again, squeezing it into a fist.

"We should go," he says abruptly.

After the rapid escalation of that kiss, I was worried I'd be churning to keep up, but his short dismissal after the hottest kiss of my life has me rooted in place. *What the hell is going on?*

As if he senses my internal struggle, he cups my elbow and steers me toward the exit.

I'm frowning at the floor, not seeing anyone we're passing, when he tilts his head toward mine. "I don't want to have to pretend about how much the happy couple means to me."

Pretend. That's right. The kiss meant nothing to him. If I was as smart as my parents raised me to be, it'd mean nothing to me, too. But as he leads me out into the dry night air, the sounds of the band fading behind us, I have to wonder if I'm safer dodging Samuel's attempts on my own.

Five

Ford

Last night, I dropped Lia off and drove straight home to take a cold shower. Only the water was lukewarm and my dick could've cut through metal as easily as the jaws of life.

That fucking wedding. That fucking photographer and her kiss cam.

It should be called a sleepless night cam. Because that's all I got after that smoking-hot kiss with Lia.

Wescott.

As if referring to her by her last name would wipe out how right she felt plastered against me, how responsive she was as soon as my mouth was on hers.

I roll out of bed and rub my eyes. I need to rub something else.

My boxers strain against my raging morning erection. Maybe it's because I haven't been laid in a while and I'm not used to waking up with a load that weighs a ton. Or maybe it's because I tossed and turned, dreaming of soft lips against my mouth and hard nipples pressing into my chest. With that dress she wore, it wouldn't have been anything to sneak her into a bathroom stall or behind the bushes or, hell, even into my car.

Lia's not like that. She's not public sex and meaningless fucks. She's classy. Sex in the bushes at my stepsister's wedding is not sophisticated.

Dammit. We left before I could congratulate Karoline. I'm sure she'll hold it against me, and it's not like I can tell her that I couldn't hold Lia through another dance and keep my body under control. When Lia said *twerking* and I pictured her ass bumping up and down, ripe enough to sink my teeth into—

Then the kiss.

I give my face one last scrub. My erection is painful now and I have no options. Okay, maybe one...

I heave my way to the bathroom. I have a full day before I work with her again. And while I'm willing to jack off in my bed like a fifteen-year-old, I can take care of business in the shower like an adult and find some relief.

I flip the water on and get in before it warms up. No help. I'm still hard enough to carve my name into a diamond. As the water heats, I palm myself, hissing at my own touch. I'm desperate. Giving my dick a pump, I let my mind wander to Lia's wide eyes and kiss-plump lips. Involuntarily, I tighten my grip.

Releasing myself with a jerk, I grab the shampoo. I can't do this. I can't jerk off to my partner. But by the time my scalp's scrubbed and rinsed, nothing's changed. My erection isn't going away.

What did I used to think about when I masturbated?

The last time was when Cass was pregnant. She felt bloated and enormous—her words—and refused to let me touch her. Before she left me and stomped on my heart—

before the big ultrasound I wasn't invited to—I used to dream about her larger breasts and the curve of her growing belly.

I hate to do it, but I wrap my hand around my dick again and stroke.

I try picturing Cass's face, but all I can see is her pout when she tells me I disappointed her. Then the way her eyes flash when she says a manwhore like me can't be a role model for her kid.

Her kid.

My grip tightens painfully.

Dammit.

Well, that takes care of my erection. I should feel like running a marathon the way blood's streaming back into my body. By the time I wash myself and do a down-and-dirty shave, the feather of Lia's lips under mine fills my brain and blood's rushing back to my groin.

Fuck.

Just get it done.

I squeeze my eyes shut and try to think of nothing but the paltry pleasure I can bring myself. Finally, I'm getting somewhere. As steam billows around me and water sluices down my hypersensitized skin, I pump my fist. A shock of red lips flashes through my brain. A firm ass bouncing up and down with gauzy yellow material swaying over flesh that has to be as creamy and smooth as the rest of her.

I grit my teeth and slam a hand against the slippery shower tile, my other hand working so furiously that the water makes a piss-poor lube. If I have a heat rash when this is over, I deserve it. I can't stop the erotic images of Lia streaming through my imagination. Her swaying backside in that dress at the country club. Her slow bend.

What would she look like naked, nothing impeding my

gaze from her narrow ankles, up her strong calves, to those thighs rounded with muscle?

Electricity tingles at the base of my spine. All I have to do is imagine slipping that same dress over her shoulders, downward, until one rosy nipple pops free. My balls tighten, and in my mind's eye, I'm lowering my head to capture one of those tight peaks that poked me in my chest. A roar rips from my chest as my climax crashes over me. Water runs into my eyes, down to my mouth, only to turn to spray as I moan and heave.

Fuck.

I sag against the wall, my stroking hand hanging limp, water washing my release away. I don't even know where I sprayed. I don't care. I'm too lost in the empty afterglow, my brain reeling over an orgasm that's stronger than any I've had since...ever.

I can't afford to think about Lia this way. She's too important to me and she's hung up on some other guy. I'll only stomp on us and ruin our friendship when she wants more. They always want more.

I've shirked relationships for so long. My only serious one ended with Cass taking the most important thing in my life. I left my career before it started for my mom. I'm pretending to date Lia for Cass so I can get that time with Jayden. Beyond that, I had no other plans.

So, where does that leave me?

As I towel off, only one question roams through my mind. *What do I want?*

∩∩

I'm getting into a pair of shorts when my phone chimes. A missed voice mail from Cass.

I hop on one foot while I finish dressing on my way to

the nightstand as fast as possible. Missing Cass's calls when I'm working annoys her enough. Not answering otherwise is a major strike against me.

I listen to the message. Just a curt "call me" and Jayden screaming in the background.

My pulse spikes as worst-case scenarios download in my imagination. Is there something wrong with him? His airway is obviously clear, but maybe he hit his head. Did he lose consciousness?

Cass answers with an irritated "Yeah?" Jayden's stuttered cries pierce my heart. I just want to fucking hold him. To comfort him when he's hurt.

"Hey. Is everything okay?"

"Yeah, why?"

Relief chases away any irritation at her attitude and helps me watch my own tone. "He was cry—nothing. What's up?"

"I have a meeting tomorrow and I need you to watch Jayden."

Aw, hell. Here we go. "I work a twelve tomorrow. It's on the schedule I gave you."

"You're his dad. Take it off."

Finding someone to cover a twelve-hour shift on this short of notice would be next to impossible. "We're short-staffed. I can try my mom—"

"Your mom hasn't touched a baby in years. Her own stepkids hate her."

We've been over this before. Besides, Jayden's a toddler. Not as fragile as a baby, but more self-destructive. "Speaking of which, we were just at Karoline's wedding."

"Were you even invited?" Cass says flatly.

"Yes. Lia and I went with Mom."

"Lia? Your partner?"

This is it. Once I tell Cass, there's no going back. She's

the reason I came up with the idea that left me twisted all damn night. "We're dating."

"Like...as in more than once?"

I wince. "Yes, Cass."

She *tsks*. "You can't even keep it in your pants at work."

I say quietly, "Lia's a good person, and I'll do what I need to do to be a good father for Jayden."

"He could've had a physician for a dad. You would've been a resident by now."

I stay silent. I've lost this argument a hundred times. It doesn't matter what I say about my decision to not apply for residency, about the dire financial straits Mom was left in. Being a paramedic when I could've been a doctor is my shame to bear in Cass's eyes.

A loud sigh resonates over the line. "Can't you at least try to get out of work during my meeting? Or don't you want your girlfriend to be partnered with anyone else?"

She sounds less catty and more vulnerable. As much as she's used my playboy ways against me, is she prepared for me to be monogamous or is my plan going to backfire? I never thought of that. Maybe she's insecure about it all. She made it clear when she broke up with me that I failed her. She's still punishing me for not spending my days trying to win her back all these years later.

I only deal with her to beg for time with Jayden.

It's paying off. She's actually asking for my help. I can't let her down now. "I'll take care of it. When are you going to bring him over?"

As she gives me the details, I make a mental list of who I can call to switch shifts with me. Will Lia think I'm avoiding her after the kiss? Our stilted goodbye when I dropped her off at her place after the wedding had to be as uncomfortable for her as it was for me. And after the shower episode, I don't know if I can work with her and ignore the fact that the fantasy of her got me off.

I could call her, but my dick is already excited that it might hear her voice. No, I'll call Mitch and see if he can trade shifts and I'll leave it up to him to let Lia know.

I should call her though.

But we're not really dating. I don't normally tell her when I switch shifts unless we happen to work together, and I know I need to trade, likewise, for her.

I get ahold of Mitch and turn my brain off when it comes to Lia. Of all people, she'll understand.

Lia

He's avoiding me.

I arrived for my shift Monday morning armed with water bottles, a packed lunch, and a stomach twisted in knots at the thought of seeing Ford. We'd be alone in the ambulance cab. Alone at our post while waiting for a call. Alone together.

Would he be aloof and cool like he was after the wedding? Could we fall into our same old groove as partners? Or had that kiss irrevocably changed things between us?

All that worry for nothing. I've spent the last eleven and a half hours with Mitch. Ford is working with Arnesh this Saturday instead.

Mitch backs the ambulance into the garage bay and I'm dutifully guiding him, surrounded by diesel fumes, but in reality, I'm distracted. Good thing Mitch has done this a thousand times and doesn't take out the garage doorframe.

Instead of switching out for driving after each run, he likes to split the shift. I've been riding shotgun since noon. Which is fine.

It's just not my routine with Ford.

Mitch punches the button to close the garage door and gets out. He catches me scowling at the ambulance. "Did I do something to piss you off, Wescott? You're acting like you got stuck on the douche crew."

A moniker we've given Russel, another paramedic who should've been fired years ago. Mitch isn't so smug he's dangerous like Russel is. "No. Why?"

His expression says the answer should be as clear as the blue lips on the emphysema patient we just left at the ER. "You've barely said a word that didn't have to do with patient care."

What is he talking about? It's been a steady day. When did Mitch and I have time to chat?

There was the hour over lunch when we had no calls. Then, the first stretch this morning, when I was lost in a cloud of wondering why Ford wasn't working. Mitch said something about Jayden, but Ford's never gotten to have his son so long that he had to take off work.

Of course a twelve-hour shift would be the first time Cass allowed it.

"Wescott." His brows are raised like he can't believe he lost me midconversation. He's given me that look more than once today.

"Sorry, no. You did nothing wrong. I like working with you, Mitch."

"But not as much as working with your boyfriend?"

I wince. I hate lying to people. Letting Samuel, my parents, Ford's mom, and his ex think we're an item is one thing, but Mitch isn't meddling family or a cheating ex. He's a nice guy and an amazing paramedic.

"It's not that." My answer sounds as weak as my resolve to keep lying to a guy I consider not just a coworker but a friend. I mean, I was at his son's graduation party last year. I traded cookie recipes with his wife.

"Did you two get in a tiff?" He says it with a joking tone, but his eyes are all serious. He's worried about me.

Guilt wells up and the truth spills out, mostly because I have no one else to talk to. Normally, I'd tell Ford since he's my closest friend. I can't talk to him about *him*, and I can't talk to anyone else because, according to the rest of the world, we're supposed to be dating.

"We're not dating," I confess. "We're pretending because his ex is on a power trip and my mother wants to control my life."

I swallow hard. Mitch stares at me, his eyes owlish and his Adam's apple bobbing as he attempts a reply. Finally, he shakes his head and lets out a wry chuckle. "I wondered why it seemed so sudden. You two were buddies and then bam! —you're dating. It was weird. Not that it doesn't make sense." His forehead crinkles. "If you want it to make sense. I don't mean that you two don't work together really well, but I didn't think you did *that* together really well." His face flushes hemoglobin red. "Hell. You know what I mean."

I don't. "Yep."

He bobs his head. "Well, your secret's safe with me, but I still don't get what that has to do with you being in your head all day." His expression turns irritated. "Is he supposed to be fake dating you, but he's seeing other women on the side?"

I could laugh at the way Mitch is ready to defend my fake honor, but the thought of Ford being with other women while we're pretending to be together makes my stomach roil. We talked about that and I trust him, but part of my brain refuses to listen to reason. "No, we established ground rules. The custody issue is pretty serious."

"I wish I was rich so I could buy that kid a lawyer. His ex wouldn't stand a chance in court and she knows it."

"Agreed." My parents both know excellent lawyers, ones who owe them favors, but they'll refuse to help because Ford is an obstacle between me and Samuel. "We went to his stepsister's wedding." I have to get this off my chest but my heart's racing. "And we had to pretend to kiss for the photographer. She wanted to get all the couples in love."

He cocks a brow. "Unless you turned your back and rubbed noses, it's kinda hard to pretend to kiss."

"Exactly."

"That good or that bad?"

That good. That fucking good. My face heats and Mitch gives me a knowing nod.

"Ford isn't the type to be bad at that stuff. So now it's awkward between you two?"

"I don't know. Yes? I thought he was avoiding me."

"He didn't tell you why he couldn't work today?"

I lift a shoulder. "I'm not his girlfriend."

"Do you want to be?"

"No," I answer before I can think, afraid of what I'd find if I ventured down that path. "It's Ford."

"We both know Ford's a good guy, or you wouldn't be friends with him."

"He is a good guy. But Cass ruined him. He wants nothing to do with relationships and the last thing I need is a guy who's tied so close to his ex."

Understanding lights Mitch's eyes. "Your ex cheated with his ex. I can see the issue." He crosses his arms, his gaze boring into the floor. "Maybe you should just ask him if that kiss made it awkward."

"Maybe." No way in hell I was bringing that up with

Ford. Getting left on the doorstep at my condo minutes after the incident dented my ego enough.

"I'm serious, Lia. My wife and I used to fight all the time. It's one of the few things I've put my foot down on. One day, I told her I can't read her mind—I'm oblivious on a good day. If she has an issue with me, she has to tell me. I can't work on what I don't know."

"Makes sense," I mumble. I told Mitch for a reason. Maybe it was because he has all the experience and therefore his advice is something I should listen to.

"Relationships have vitals, but I went to school for this job. There is no class for relationships. I guess there is, but you know what I mean. Instead of a stethoscope, we have to talk to know how stable we are. Just remember, you two work well together for a reason. Whether it's work ethic, respect, or chemistry, it doesn't matter. You'll work it out."

Chemistry. I never thought I had chemistry with Ford. I diligently kept myself from thinking about him that way, from appreciating his wide shoulders and powerful thighs. When we were first paired together, I ignored my insides tingling every time he complimented me. He's a player. I knew that from the beginning.

Then why does it suddenly seem so hard to ignore all those things now? It's like my mind's rewinding and replaying every time he grinned at me, all the inside jokes we share, how he warms me to the point of intimate discomfort. The thing we had going is messed up over an amazing kiss.

Mitch glances to the door where the new team is entering and heading to the locker room. "I wanted to talk to you about something before we go."

"Okay?"

"Did you see that the company is offering a paramedic course this fall?"

"I figured they would be. Isn't it an every-other-year

thing?" When I first moved here, I chose only to do the shorter EMT course. It was an entirely new career and I had to feel it out first.

"The pay increase would be significant."

I'm not worried about the money. "Worried that I'll lose the roof over my head?"

"No, but we're talking dollars more an hour. You're an excellent EMT, and you'd be a great paramedic. Not many places offer an accelerated program—and pay for it."

His tone says I would be a fool to pass this up. It's a great opportunity. So why am I so reluctant to listen to Mitch on this? Perhaps I want to decide for myself. I moved here determined to make my own way, to carve my own path in the world, and I'm doing that.

I'm doing exactly what I moved to Fargo to do. And Ford is helping me keep it that way.

When I don't express the excitement Mitch expects of me, he says, "Is it the three-year contract?"

"I don't know. I haven't thought about it that hard." Three years working for the same company after the course was done. Since the course doesn't start until September, I'd be committing to at least four years—to both this company and Fargo.

Four years.

I came here with no plan, but four years sounds like more than a plan. Four more years living next to Mrs. Rosenthal. Four more years renting. I can hear Dad spouting his financial advice when I graduated from college.

Why would you throw money away on a rental when you can start building equity?

Instead of throwing my money away, I moved in with Samuel. Into the house he'd shared with his ex-wife, into the same bedroom.

"Just keep it in mind. We want you to stick around."

Mitch lifts his chin toward the two incoming crew members leaving the locker room.

As he launches into the details of our shift and the unusual ticking he thinks he heard from the engine, I let my mind drift. A paramedic. Ford did the accelerated class when he got out of medical school. He's almost done with his three-year contract. He also told me I should go the same route. I was too new and feeling over my head during my first few months on the job to listen then.

Getting my job to pay for the course while guaranteeing work for the near future is a good deal. I'd even be able to work part-time while doing classes.

We want you to stick around.

Since Mitch has his eye on the manager position, he's got the company's best interests in mind, not just mine. I'm a little tired of people with ulterior motives making decisions for me. I'll table that discussion for now.

Unfortunately, that leaves his earlier advice to talk to Ford.

How would I do that? Wait until our next shift on Thursday? No, my private life has encroached on work too much already.

So that leaves calling him or stopping over, but since he doesn't answer his phone half the time unless it's Cass or his mom, that leaves going to his place.

That won't be awkward at all.

∩∩

I changed into a pair of jean shorts and a pink T-shirt before I left work. But as I'm walking up to Ford's door, I can't help tugging at the hemline. Maybe I should've put on something nicer? This was all I had and it's just fine. I don't want him to get the wrong idea. I'm here as a friend, worried about our friendship.

The door looms before me, a battered wood door that Ford is saving up to replace. He's put so much money into his childhood home, upgrading plumbing, fixing the fence to keep the neighbor's dog from crapping in his yard, and replacing appliances as they died from old age, that the door is low on the priority list.

Maggie's so proud of all the work he's done. She's renting an apartment only a few blocks away. Ford is tied forever to Fargo with this old house, but Maggie Monroe can pick up stakes and move whenever.

Another reason to admire Maggie. What she went through was so much worse than me, but we're both carving our own path.

I open the screen door and knock, then clench my hands together. This is Ford. I shouldn't be so nervous about visiting him. It's just a talk. All I have to ask is *Hey, are we cool?*

A shriek sounds from the other side of the door. *Oh, crap.* Jayden's still over. I assumed that Cass wouldn't let Ford have him for more than a couple of hours, and since this is when he'd normally be off work, now she'd conveniently not need him to watch Jayden.

Crap, crap, crap. Maybe he didn't hear the knock. Can I leave without him knowing I was here?

The door flies open. Concern fills Ford's gaze. "Lia. Is something wrong?"

Because I'm not usually here unless his car is broken down. That's still coworker status. I don't just drop by.

"I'm sorry, I didn't mean to bother you. I can come back another time." A phone call is going to be more awkward after this, but I'll have time to think of something. Something work related. Something definitely not about that kiss.

Gah! I feel wrong even thinking about it when his son is right behind him.

"No, no. Actually, this works really well. Cass is supposed to be here in a few minutes to pick him up and I told her we were dating."

That answers the "Are we okay?" question. He's still on board with the fake dating.

This means that he really only took off work to watch his son and our kiss didn't affect him a bit.

Well, I've got my answer. "Are you sure you want me around when she comes?"

At the sound of a crash behind him, he whips around. "Don't worry, buddy. We'll put the Legos back together." He focuses back on me, his gaze dipping down my outfit and lingering on my legs. His look is as good as a caress. Shivers cascade down my back.

"We've been playing this game for the last half hour," Ford says, not missing a beat. "It's one where I build up a tower of those big Legos, or Duplos—whatever—and he knocks it down. Why don't you come inside?"

Crossing the threshold feels too much like I'm entering the ring, missing all the preparation I need for battle. Hearing that we're dating is different than seeing me in Ford's house.

The plus side is that Cass never deigned this place worthy enough for her. Too small. Too old. She was house hunting before Ford even graduated. Only the houses she liked were for a pediatrician who'd already paid off his school loans, not a new grad going into residency.

"What's up?" Ford stands on the welcome mat just inside his door, a tiny pair of athletic shoes next to his big, bare feet.

I jerk my gaze up before I can contemplate how nice his feet are, long and strong, so much like the rest of him.

They're just feet. Oops. Guess I wasn't fast enough. "You weren't at work today."

He gestures toward Jayden. The boy's fisting giant red Duplo bricks in each hand. "Cass called at the last minute. Mitch saved me."

I ducked my head. "He mentioned that you were spending the day with Jayden."

His brow crinkles, a question in his eyes. If Mitch told me why Ford was missing work, then why am I here?

I blow out a gusty breath. "I was just worried things were awkward between us, you know, after..."

Understanding dawns in his blue gaze. "No. No, it's not awkward. I should've called. It's just that I don't usually when I take a day off."

Absolutely. Because we aren't dating.

Feeling more foolish by the minute, I shuffle my feet and peek at the kid. Jayden's too young to follow our conversation, but it still feels weird talking like this around him. "I just wanted to make sure we're cool. Are you sure I should stick around for Cass? I don't want to ruin any progress you've made."

"She's the one that wanted this."

He lifts his gaze to monitor what Jayden's doing. The loose T-shirt and basketball shorts are so much different than Ford's normal look. Our uniforms are barriers and not just for bodily fluids. When we're each dressed in our polo and tactical pants, it's a clear signal to our brains that we're working.

The wedding dance was different. His mom was there and we were out. Now I'm in his house, waiting to meet the mom of his kid. I know all about Cass, but I've never been introduced to her. She won't come near the ambulance garage and I doubt we hang out in the same places.

"Since she's the main reason why we're doing this"—he sweeps his hand out—"have a seat."

I pad forward, my footsteps swallowed by the banging of plastic blocks. Jayden has zero interest in me and since I have no clue what to do with kids and this visit is turning out more momentous than planned, I'm okay with that.

After dropping onto a surprisingly comfortable couch, I stick my hands between my knees to keep from fidgeting. I don't know how else to act and that's the last feeling I'm used to around Ford.

Ford doesn't take a seat next to me but drops onto the floor next to his son. "Jayden, this is my friend Lia." Jayden gnaws on a block. Ford smirks. "He says hi. How was the shift?"

"Pretty normal."

"Normal's good."

"Yeah."

Is this conversation only one-sidedly painful, or is he cringing on the inside, too?

To make it worse, the doorbell rings. We both tense and Jayden waves his little arms around.

"That's probably her." He unfolds his big body and I can't bring myself to ogle him as he goes to the door. "Hey."

"Sorry, the meeting ran long and since it was a video, I couldn't text you without being obvious." Cass breezes past him, shoving her aviator sunglasses on top of her perfectly windblown blond hair. Her suit manages to look chic and professional at the same time. She's paired wide-legged black pants with a loose suit jacket that's not meant to button. Her cream shirt is expertly knotted above the waist. All she has to do is strike a pose with her hands in her pockets and she could walk right out of a fashion magazine.

She stops short when she sees me. "Oh." Emotions play across her face, every one playing through her green eyes.

Confusion. Surprise. A hotter emotion bordering on anger, then grim acceptance. "Lia?"

I rise and stretch out a hand. Ford is in shorts and a T-shirt too, but I feel sorely underdressed. "Hi, Cass. Finally, we meet."

"Right. Finally." Her hand clasps mine for a millisecond before she snatches it away. She turns and squats in front of Jayden. "Hey, buddy. How was playing at Daddy's?"

Ford produces a diaper bag from behind the couch. "He cut his nap an hour short, so he's been kind of cranky."

"An hour?" Cass lets out a long-suffering sigh. "It's that thing you use. It's not his crib."

"I tried laying him down with me, but he was just distracted."

"I guess he'll have to go to bed early tonight. I hope he doesn't also wake up early since his sleep schedule's thrown off."

She might just be voicing her concerns, but her tone makes it clear that it'll be all Ford's fault.

My phone chooses that moment to start buzzing. Vibrate is not silent and it echoes between the three of us. Four, if I count Jayden, but he's more interested in the shoes Cass is trying to stuff on his feet.

I'm tempted to ignore it, but I don't get many calls and my curiosity wins. My parents or Samuel?

My mom. "Excuse me."

I give Cass a quick smile, but she eyes me like I've failed some unknown test she was conducting.

I shoot an apologetic look at Ford. He shakes his head like it's no problem, but his shoulders hang like he knows he's failed his own test. He should also know that it wouldn't matter. I'm sure seeing me amped up Cass's Ford-criticism factor.

Ducking into the hallway, I answer. "Hello?"

"Aurelia. Hi." Mom's businesslike tone drifts over the line. I imagine her dressed much like Cass, only with a properly mature tucked-in blouse and her highlighted walnut hair in a French twist. "Listen, your father and I are going to be in North Dakota this weekend."

"What?" They haven't been here since Grandma died. Mrs. Rosenthal evicted her deadbeat tenant when she heard I needed a place to stay. I'd have been on my own if I had needed movers too. It was my parents' passive-aggressive way of teaching me a lesson.

It's only thanks to Mrs. Rosenthal and her nose for good deals that I even have some furniture.

"Yes, dear. We haven't been out there to see you yet and I have a break in my campaign schedule." She means she *made* a break in her campaign schedule. Mom's job as a California state senator is her identity. Campaigning is critical and her priority every election season. There's no such thing as a "break" in September. Which means I won't like the reason for the visit. "Samuel tells me you're seeing someone."

There it is.

"Yes." I don't give her more. She talks to him more than she talks to me. I know they've worked together and she's his mentor. It didn't bother me as much when I was with Samuel, but the resentment is building more each day I'm gone.

Mom and I don't have much in common. I went to school in a field she loved. At the time, I thought it was because my life was so steeped in politics, I must be destined for it. But the longer I'm in Fargo. The more times I have lemonade on Mrs. Rosenthal's back porch, with the smell of citronella in the air, and evade her nosy questions about the patients I deal with. The more I realize that I must have wanted a link to Mom. Now that I'm not following in her footsteps, what else do we have to talk about?

"Is he the man you've been working with?" Mom's voice invades my swell of disappointment.

"I'm sure whatever Samuel told you is accurate."

"Aurelia, don't be like that."

How often have I heard that from her? Whenever I don't act like her, she says it. Yet I recite my standard response. "Like what, Mom?"

"Immature. You're twenty-five. Samuel is a nice young man with a good head on his shoulders. I wish you knew what you walked away from."

"He's a cheater."

"He's human and he loves you."

Thank God I have a lie to fall back on. "I'm with Ford now."

"A man that took advantage of a younger and inexperienced partner."

"He's a nice young man with a good head on his shoulders." Yes, that was immature. But I don't have many tools to deal with my parents, especially Mom. It's either obedient acquiescence or petty remarks.

Mom's sigh is so familiar it propels me back to my teenage years. Hell, I don't even have to go back that far. She made the same noise when I told her I was leaving both her campaign team and San Francisco. Right before she said, *Aurelia, don't be like that.* "Your father and I would like to meet him. We're your parents. We worry."

Thirsty for more signs that Mom cares about me and not just me and Samuel, I can't refuse her outright. "He works Saturday." I hope she doesn't catch that I only said *he.*

"Then we'll meet on Sunday. Samuel said the country club is adequate."

The country club. Where it all started. "Let me know

what time and we'll be there," I say before we hang up. I just have to make sure Ford can and will make it.

When I walk back out to the living room, Cass has Jayden on her hip and she's inches away from Ford, speaking so low I can't make out a word she's saying.

Ford's planted his hands on his hips, his stormy expression wiping away any creeping jealousy regarding their proximity. Samuel and his ex-wife used to talk like that. She'd stop by the house with some urgent reason to meet with him and I'd find them standing toe to toe, her earnest expression too hopeful to be about how the electric company won't take his name off her account, so she can't fix an overcharge.

"Sorry. Bad time?" I ask, shaking off old memories. Cass is pissed. This isn't about a simple overcharge.

Cass clenches her jaw shut but keeps glaring at Ford. "No. I was just leaving."

She yanks the diaper bag from his hand and storms out.

"See ya, buddy." He calls to Jayden and waves. Then he watches her leave, his jaw rigid.

I tuck my hands into my back pockets. "She took it that well?"

"I think it's that you're here when Jayden's around and I didn't tell her."

I want to fire back with, "Yeah, well, does she have dudes over and not tell you?" but I keep it in. If we were working together, I would. This is different. We're not coworkers right this minute and I'm the girl she's upset about. "I'm sorry."

"If it wasn't you, she'd be pissed about someone else." He rubs a hand down his face. "Anyway, I think she's more pissed because she can't find fault with you."

Ford talked about me that much with her? No, she's just done her homework. Easy enough. A quick search on me and my parents would show her everything but the last year or so and that she'd know from Ford. "The intro's over. There's that at least."

His smile is weary. "There's that."

"But we still have my parents. And guess what? They want to meet you."

"Okay." He goes to the pile of blocks and starts picking up.

"Sunday."

"What's that?"

Perhaps he can't hear me over the clatter of toys. I raise my voice. "They're coming Sunday."

Slowly, he turns. "I have to meet Elaine and Jensen Wescott that soon? Are we going to get a punch card for the country club?"

"Three fake dates and the fourth is free."

He smirks but falls quiet. I'm afraid he's going to pass and leave me to explain why my new boyfriend flaked out. It'd be easy to go back to the way we were before. Tell everyone that nope, we didn't work out, but hey, we're still friends. I'm already rehearsing the speech in my head.

Finally, he says, "I guess if we have to go on this call, we'll do lights and sirens all the way. What time?"

Seven

Ford

Is this what Lia felt when she was waiting in my house for Cass to arrive? My palms are sweaty, I've checked my hair in every window and reflective surface on the way here, and I have a strong urge to run.

I wasn't this nervous when I met Cass's parents. I was almost excited. Serious about Cass, I'd been intent on making a good impression. But there are so many differences between then and today.

The primary one being that Lia and I aren't a real couple.

But despite all the differences, there's one thing that feels all too familiar. I've been down this road before—and I crashed and burned.

From everything Lia said, her parents are doppelgängers for Mr. and Mrs. Pruitt. Image, prestige, and the social circles they run in define their lives, and all of those parameters extend to their only child.

I've heard a lot about Samuel over the last year and met him only briefly, but we're worlds apart. He has blue blood, lofty ambitions, and connections I'll never have—and that I don't care to have. When I left a career as a physician and signed up with Fargo EMS, I never would've guessed that the desire to save lives doesn't rank very high with some people.

I pull up to the curb in front of Lia's place. The drapes in Mrs. Rosenthal's windows twitch. I can't see her, but I wave anyway. Lia's out the door before I come to a stop, wearing a simple black cocktail dress that hugs all the essentials and hints at the rest. I barely have time to put the vehicle in park before she gets in.

"They're there already."

"But we're not meeting for a half hour yet." It takes ten minutes to get to the country club from Lia's place. I've never been late in my life, but Lia's said before that on time is late in her parents' world.

"They got to town early and figured we'd just magically arrive because we obviously have nothing else going on." The exasperated bitterness in her voice is a thousand times worse than any other time she's talked about her parents.

"It's a test?" I ask as I pull away.

"Probably." She clutches her hands in her lap, the rest of her body also rigid.

I reach the corner and, on a whim, I take a turn in the opposite direction of the country club.

Lia frowns and points behind us. "Um, that's the road we need to take."

"We're playing this different." The more I think about it, the more I like my plan. "They already don't like me. I'm not Samuel. So we're not going to kill ourselves trying to please them. We stroll in on the hour, or even five minutes late, and we pretend that it's no big deal."

"I told them we're on our way."

I take another turn down a tree-lined boulevard. We pass more houses just like the one on Lia's street. Neutral tone, white trim, with an occasional twin home between them. "We are."

She stares at me, but I only glance at her before turning back to the road. A strangled noise turns into a chuckle. She relaxes and cracks the window. "I'm going to pay for it, so you'd better make sure I enjoy it."

That's a challenge I want to rise to in the worst and most wicked way possible. But that's not what she means, so I kick my mind out of the gutter and cruise town.

I leave the residential streets and we enter a more industrial section of town. We pass a large warehouse and she says exactly what I'm thinking. "Remember the guy that fell off the roof?"

"That was a bad call." I wasn't sure we'd get him to the hospital in time for him to be life-flighted to a trauma center. Both of us worked our asses off to keep him with us.

"Did you see the last note his wife sent?"

"That he took his first steps?" The doctors didn't think he'd walk again.

"Yeah." She rests her head against the seat. "I rush to please my parents and get all worked up when I really just need to remember the cookies we get every month because a family still has their husband and dad."

"Five minutes late then?"

Her grin is sly. "Make it ten."

∩∩

We stroll into the country club like we just came back from the lake, well vacationed and reluctant to enter the hectic fray of everyday life.

We're five minutes late on the dot and Lia's phone has been blowing up for the last twenty. I took her mind off our tardiness by showing her a few of the places I ran around when I was growing up.

The park on my end of town where I coached boys' soccer during high school. The pool I used to lifeguard at. My old elementary school. I didn't think she'd be so interested, but for the last half hour, she's been laughing at stories of me running and getting dunked at the pool by the first team of seven-year-olds I ever coached. She only paused once to send her mother a text reassuring her that we were on our way.

As we stroll into the country club dining room, I have no problem picking out Lia's parents in the crowd: the mutinous couple with flat lines for mouths and eyes pinched with worry and aggression.

Lia looks more like her mom, and if she'd stayed in the world of politics, she might've developed the same fan of lines around her eyes from either scowling when things didn't go her way or forcing a smile on those she thought could advance her career. The demeanor of the woman, even from across the room, is nothing like her daughter's, but I have no trouble picturing a younger Lia mimicking her mother in that world. They're doubles, but only one version is correct, and it isn't the rubbing-elbows Lia.

Her dad, with his thinning hair trimmed short and wire-framed glasses, wears such a frown I wonder if he ever smiles. He definitely doesn't when he spots us entering the restaurant. His brow drops further and he looks like he's ready to give Lia a good scolding for worrying her mother.

She stiffens against my side. I squeeze tighter for a second, still marveling at how she fits next to me, and murmur, "Relax," moving my lips as little as possible.

She does, but it's so infinitesimal I can only tell because she's tucked into my side.

As we near the table, her dad rises, but her mom continues to sit, her expression getting frostier by the second.

"Mom, Dad, sorry we're late." She stops short of the table. Neither parent moves to greet her with a hug or a kiss. I have a feeling that's standard practice.

My mom had the cards stacked against her, but she was, and still is, affectionate.

"Yes," Mr. Wescott rumbles. "Why *were* you late?"

I have no doubt Lia's going to make up some reason on the fly and it won't make sense and shit will get awkward. So I laugh and smooth down the tie I loosened on the way inside. "Oh, you know how it is, Your Honor. State secrets."

Mr. Wescott opens his mouth to say something, but he must decide he doesn't really have anything to add. He snaps his mouth shut and sits, smoothing his own impeccable tie. I busy myself with helping Lia get settled.

"So," Lia says once she's in her chair and I'm seated. It's a shame to cover up that body with the table, but fake dating or not, I'm not going to ogle a man's daughter in front of him. "This is Ford."

I'm sure introductions would've been much more pretentious had we been on time, and they would've found a way to insinuate that I'm so far beneath them I shouldn't have tried looking at their daughter. I've never met them, but I've met enough people like them. The Pruitts and all of their friends. But Lia's parents don't know how to react when the control is taken from them. They've been on top for too many years.

Her mother's withering gaze lands on me, but I give her my best congenial smile, the one I use to approach a patient who clearly wants me to leave and take the police and fire department with me. "I'd ask what you do and how you two met, but I guess we know the answer."

"It's all there in the Star of Life," I joke and I'm met with blank stares. I gesture to my chest where the emblem would sit on my work shirt. "It's the thing we wear— It doesn't matter. Yep, we met at work."

The server stops by and I let Lia order first. The judge orders for his wife, an old-fashioned move for a woman who holds a lot of power in their relationship. But hey, whatever works for them.

When Lia orders the chicken alfredo, her mom touches her arm. "The carbs, dear."

Lia blanches and glances down at the menu, a deer-in-the-headlights look on her face.

"It's amazing," I interject, and Lia's gaze jerks up to mine. "The alfredo is awesome. Promise to let me have a bite?"

Several expressions pass over her face and I read every one. Shock and relief that I stepped in, and chagrin that she didn't realize she was caving to her hypercritical mother's wishes.

"That's a promise." She smiles, the one she gets when she lands on a valid reason for treatment that an argumentative patient didn't think of. "Want to split dessert, too?"

∩∩

Lia

Dinner is almost over, and despite half joking about sharing a dessert, Ford pores over the sweets menu with me and we select a cheesecake bite sampler.

Mom tries to intervene, saying that she and Dad are

taking off soon. That only made Ford ask for a double order to go. *Cuz we'll be hungrier later.*

I didn't realize I'd fallen for Mom's food policing until Ford defended me. I'm more horrified to think that I put up with it for years, well into adulthood, pretty much until I moved.

Samuel, for all his faults, always encouraged me to stand up to her and shut down her fine criticisms, but he also never defended me in front of her. All through dinner, Ford was downright obnoxious in his support of me. I needed it. I got the pasta dish and ate every noodle except the ones I shared with Ford.

My parents drive past us out of the parking lot as we wave. Ford grins and throws his whole arm into it as he clings to two to-go boxes with the other.

"That wasn't so bad," he says as my perturbed parents drive away. They have a flight out in two hours.

"It was awful. I'm so sorry."

"It was nothing compared to meeting the Pruitts and then dealing with them after I moved back to Fargo and Cass came with me. I might've been a little bit of a jackass today though." We walk to his car. He takes off his suit coat and flings it into the back seat. "I didn't go overboard, did I?"

"Are you kidding?" I slip into the passenger seat and sink into the scent that is Ford, which is seeped into every surface of the vehicle, a combination of Irish Spring and plain shaving cream. Ford's presence overpowers most women. He doesn't need to add a heavy cologne to it. "You had every right to be worse. It was embarrassing how they acted." I snicker before dropping my voice in imitation. "'It was either my mom on the street or me in an ambulance rig, and any idiot could make that decision.'"

Dad deserved it. He'd made a pointed comment about throwing so much money away for nothing.

"You know how many times I've wanted to say that over the last few years?" he asks.

Every time he's around Cass and her parents. I sneak a glance at him. Strong profile. Blue eyes glowing under the high sun. His tie got looser over the course of the dinner until its loop was hanging halfway down his chest.

He gives me a devilish grin. "Where to now?"

"I've wasted enough of your Sunday. You can take me home."

"Come on, we have the goods. Let's celebrate our victory. We've come up against Cass and the judge—who has nothing on your mom, by the way." Like before, he makes a turn I'm not expecting, one that'll take us away from my place. "We're supposed to be dating. We should be seen in more places together than the country club."

A thrill sings through my belly, a reaction that's happening the more I get Ford to myself. "Where are we going?"

"Remember the park I showed you earlier?"

"Dressed like this?"

"Why not? People will think it's romantic."

It is romantic. That's the problem. Facing Cass—not romantic. Meeting my parents—not romantic. Finding out he's an expert kisser—hot. Add a picnic in the park while dressed up and my mind's going to have a hard time convincing my heart that this will be over as soon as Ford can convince Cass to give him more time with his son and my parents lay off about Samuel.

Still, I don't want to go home. "If you can find a picnic table that's not covered in bird shit, then sure."

"No table. I have a blanket in the trunk."

Dismay leaves a sour taste in my mouth. This experience

might be new to me—Samuel wasn't prone to romantic gestures—but I have a feeling Ford has a blanket that might glow under a black light. "I'll risk the grass."

"Wait—do you think I'm such a manwhore that I'll whip out a blanket and head to the park whenever I can't go back to her place?"

I hate the nameless and faceless *her* in this scenario, but I get over it. I've insulted him, thinking the worst of him like everyone else in his life. "Sorry."

"I'd have washed it if that was the case. But no, the blanket has never been fucked on. I tossed it in when I drove back and forth from Grand Forks. I have an entire emergency winter survival kit in my trunk."

He told me once that he'd come back a lot when his stepfather was sick. He'd clean the house and take care of the yardwork so his mom could sit at the hospital. "I didn't mean to assume."

"I've earned it."

Grim acceptance. He has a reputation, yes, but I know him better than those girls. I know him better than anyone but Maggie.

We don't say much more as he maneuvers through the park and finds a spot where we'll have some privacy. I'm not sure how far this'll go to show everyone we're dating, but after pretending for others so much, I want him to myself. Learning about him is different when it's more than just coworker chat. He's even more three-dimensional than he was before.

He retrieves the blanket and I gather the food.

There's a large tree that's perfect for sitting under near the parking lot. If he had parked on the other end, we'd need to walk half a mile to this spot, but given he's so familiar with the area from his coaching days, he saved my feet from blisters. I pick my way across the grass and kick off my heels next to the spread-out fabric.

It's no cheap item, either. The plush fleece over manicured grass is divine after a few hours in these shoes. I can't believe I used to spend so much time in them between college and my EMT days. Give me my boots any day.

He takes my armload and I sink down, folding my legs next to me to avoid flashing my most private parts. I can't wear much for underwear in this dress. So, no underwear.

I expect to pick at my goodies and restrain myself from ravaging it all, but he plucks out a chocolate chip cheesecake bite instead and holds it out for me. Like I'm supposed to eat it from his fingers.

His lips curl into a challenging smirk. He doesn't think I'll do it.

I narrow my eyes and lean forward. Since this isn't something I've ever done, I overshoot and my lips close around the tips of his fingers.

Enjoying the beat of surprise and the heat that infuses his gaze, I suck as I pull the bite into my mouth. I might've gone too far.

My face heats as I chew. To cover my reaction, I hold up a piece of strawberry swirl. His eyes darken. He's not going to hesitate. The question is, will he stop at the food?

Eight

Ford

What the fuck did I just do?

I only meant to tease Lia, to see if she'd back away, embarrassed. But this is a woman who left a privileged family and a promising career in politics to rush into a ditch and wrap a tourniquet around a motorcyclist's amputated leg.

No way would she back down.

Did I count on that?

But when those lips of hers hit my finger, I knew nothing but the wet, pink flesh on my skin and the soft sweep of her tongue. How much better would it be if I had that mouth on more of me?

Now she's presenting me with an opportunity to taunt her right back?

Game on.

My gaze captures hers and her eyes flare as I dip my head,

holding eye contact. I purposely overshoot the cheesecake bite and wrap my lips around her fingertips and suck.

The explosion of sweet dessert over my tongue mixes with Lia's soft gasp and I'm lost. Every neuron in my brain remembers how she tasted and I want more.

The cheesecake's forgotten as I lean in, releasing her fingers and swallowing the bite without chewing.

I push her back and capture her mouth before her back hits the blanket. I don't waste time licking across her lips. I want in. I want more of Lia.

She whimpers and opens for me. I dive in. Her arms twine around my neck, but I'm all gentleman—I don't roll on top of her and wedge myself between her legs. With the dress she's wearing, she'd give everyone way more of a show than we're already giving them.

I've been fighting the realization that there are no panty lines under that snug dress. I'm more than aware of it now.

Our tongues lap at each other, tasting the sugar, the need and the desire. She's as eager as I am. A groan escapes and I sink down over her. I love the feel of her body against mine. She's solid, and for once, I don't worry that I might be too big, too heavy, too much.

I don't know how long we kiss. I let my hands roam up and down her sides, stroking from under her breast and over the curve of her waist to her strong thigh. It's there that my fingers graze bare, satiny skin.

I don't care how many women I've been with. Nothing has made me feel more like I've got no damn experience than anticipating what else I'll get to touch. I'm looking forward to it more than my first time getting past first base.

I curl my hands around the hem and my arms tense, holding her in place.

Dammit, but I can't haul her dress up and get to the place I want to touch the most. We're in public.

I'm not the only one who's noticed.

"Excuse me," a male voice interrupts.

I start at the interruption but take my time releasing her mouth. She looks at me, her lids heavy, her lips swollen from mine. I'm dying to take control of them again, but I have some dickwad to tell *fuck you very much*.

I'm hard as stone and can't completely roll over without flashing more than a bulge, and I need to protect Lia from some idiot's gawking. I crane my neck to glare over my shoulder. "What the he—" *Shit*.

I get an eyeful of navy-blue pants and black boots. The sun's shining behind his head, but I still know Officer Nelson when I see him. He's not a bad guy, but why couldn't it have been some dad telling us to cool off because kids were playing?

"Monroe, not surprised to see it's you," he drawls. His gaze shifts and his eyes flare. He blinks a few times. "Wescott?"

I suppress a growl and roll onto my ass, keeping my knees bent until blood evacuates my groin.

Lia sits up and primly adjusts her skirt, hiding that creamy flesh I only got to touch briefly. "Hey, Nelson."

"So, you two are, uh..."

I bristle at the confusion in his voice. Is it so crazy that Lia would settle for someone like me? Or that I'd settle down at all? Hell, if I was ever going to do long term again, I'd be lucky if she was half Lia's caliber.

"We are, yeah," Lia answers and glances at me. She runs a hand over that glorious hair. My chest puffs in pride. Her glossy strands are messed up because of me.

"Oh. Wow." Nelson's voice continues to ring with disbelief despite catching us making out. "I mean, I heard talk, but I didn't believe it."

"Well, now you know," I snap.

Lia's brow crinkles, but she lifts her gaze to the officer. "Is something wrong?"

Nelson relaxes. "Not as long as you keep your clothes on. I stopped to eat my lunch and a mom flagged me down. She was afraid any kids playing nearby would get an eyeful."

I wouldn't let anyone see that much of Lia, adult or otherwise.

But Nelson keeps going, souring my mood even further. "Since it's you, Lia, I'm not worried." He sticks a finger in my direction. "This guy, though…"

Her casual chuckle sounds forced before drifting away.

Nelson's laugh dies off. It's not like joking around when we're Monroe and Wescott. We're Ford and Lia, dating. This discomfort must be why people don't tell their coworkers they're dating.

He runs his hand down the back of his neck. "So anyway, behave yourselves, all right? And…congratulations?"

"Yeah, thanks," I say, glad to see his back as he wanders toward the parking lot opposite where I parked.

I prepare myself for the ultimate tirade, a torrent of blame for the predicament I got us into, and chance a look at Lia. Her mortified expression wavers, then her lips curl. A quiet giggle grows louder and prompts my own laugh.

She covers her face with her hands, her shoulders shaking as she laughs outright. "God, that's what getting caught is like?"

"Don't tell me you've never been busted making out."

She rolls her eyes, but her smile stays in place. "How often have you been caught?"

"In high school, college, or as an adult?"

"Ford!" She gives me a playful swat, but I catch her arm and pull her close.

Her breath hitches and her gaze snags on my mouth, like

she's remembering how it was all over her only a few moments ago. I know I can't forget it. "Tell me, Wescott. When'd you learn how to kiss like that?"

An adorable crinkle lines her forehead. "What do you mean? I'm not the one with the tongue the girls whisper about in the feminine products aisle."

"Just because you've never heard guys talking about you doesn't mean it hasn't happened."

She lifts a brow. "I've only made out once where people could see and it was with a girl—"

I jerk her closer. "Don't tease a guy like that, not after he's been warned by the cops to keep it in his pants."

"He said to keep it in your pants *in public.*"

My mind stalls. I'm sure she's teasing me again, but could it also be an invitation to bare it all with her in private? Because one brush of her skin against mine will never be enough. I *have* to know what the rest of her is like. What she feels like, what she tastes like. How she sounds when she's— My pants grow uncomfortable once again. "Does that mean we should do this...privately?"

We both go still. Pretending to date is one thing. But we've kissed. Twice now. I want more. Does she?

Her mouth works like she's trying to form the word "no."

"We..." She lifts her chin, resolve settling into her soft-brown eyes. "We're both adults."

"And it's just sex," I say cautiously, testing the water, not believing that we've made it this far in the conversation.

She nods once, then hits me with her direct stare, the one I know from work. She's deferring to me. Casual sex is my wheelhouse, not hers.

Casual sex isn't something I'd ever associate with Lia. But right now, the only other option is no sex with Lia and that's unacceptable.

Still, she's important to me. Sex has a way of fucking important things up.

"We'd just be sleeping together," she says. "It'd help us with our, you know, pretending."

"Do you think you can sleep with me while we're pretending to date and we can still work together and be friends?" I can't keep the skepticism out of my voice.

"Do you think *you* can?" she fires back.

My hand doesn't leave her arm. I slide it down to hers and discreetly press it against the bulging fly of my pants. "Do you think I have enough blood in my brain to answer that?"

She doesn't draw her hand back. Instead, her pupils dilate and she sucks in a breath. Her fingers spread under mine to cup my manhood.

I groan and rock my hips only a little, Officer Nelson's warning echoing in my ears.

"I think we're both interested in what it'll be like. And we're both remaining abstinent otherwise." She rolls her lower lip between her teeth and I can't help straining my cock against her hand. "And I miss sex."

She's slaying me with every word out of her lush mouth.

I lift her hand, draw her index finger into my mouth, and swirl my tongue over the tip. She leans closer, and if I keep going, we're going to spread out and get the cops called on us again.

"Tell me, Lia—when's the last time you had sex?"

Again, she surprises me by answering. No coy evasion. "Sex, or when I last orgasmed?"

A ragged moan rips out of my chest. This girl is killing me. "Both."

"Last year and last night."

I make the decision before we can both come to our senses. "Then it's time to do both at the same time."

Lia

I can't agree more. Yet it's the worst idea in the history of coworkers.

Only Ford and I aren't just coworkers anymore. We kissed. We made out. We could stop here and go no further. Our time together at work would only be minimally affected.

Or would it? Ford never came on duty gushing about his conquests. He's mentioned being on a date, he's expressed his frustration that he and his dates rarely stay on the same page as far as expectations go, and sometimes he jokes with the guys about his playboy status.

It didn't seem like much at the time. Until Officer Nelson made that comment today and jealousy reared its ugly head inside me. A little voice whispered that Samuel and his ex wasn't an isolated incident. But a direct reflection that I'm not enough. I'm not enough to wipe a man's ex from his mind and I'm not enough to keep him.

But I'm not *that* girl, and I won't let Samuel's impulsive, shitty decision affect me now.

Sex with Ford sounds like a good time. Even better, it sounds like a way to forget my ex and prove to myself that I'm ready to move on.

We stare at each other for a moment, then Ford flips the lid of the crumpled cheesecake box. He doesn't feed me but pops a marbled bite into his mouth and nudges the container toward me. I pick one that's probably carrot and chew slowly. Yep. Carrot. A predictable flavor for an unpredictable situation.

"I've never done this before," he finally says.

"A relationship that's just sex?" That makes two of us.

"You're more than sex, Lia," he says softly. "That makes this more like friends with benefits, except I don't want to lose the friends part."

"The only way that'd happen is if one of us falls for the other and the other doesn't feel the same way. So we have to be honest about this."

"You think you can keep yourself from falling hard for me?" He smirks, but it's not a jest at my expense. He doesn't think I'd go for a guy like him.

I'd go for a guy exactly like him, but he's always been off-limits, and really, he still is. Cass isn't only his past. She'll always be his present and future because of Jayden. Fargo is my place to regroup. To figure out what I want to do in life. How I want to contribute. It's Ford's home. His long-term plan. He risked his future to stay here. This town became his future and as long as Jayden is here, so is Ford. Cass isn't leaving anytime soon because she's hoping to reconcile with him.

Only he won't, not after what she did with the birth certificate. The irony is that if she moves, he'll follow. Maggie's doing okay and his son is the most important person in his life. But he's not getting back together with Cass, so she's not leaving.

"It would've happened by now." The sense that I'm lying snakes through me. My inflection makes all the difference. It hasn't happened "by now" because we both purposefully avoided it.

The humor fades from his face. "No, you're right. You wouldn't have gone for a workingman like me."

"Good lord, Ford. Don't spout Cass's nonsense to me."

"What was your type before Samuel, other than the girl you kissed that I'd bet my paycheck was probably a bet you couldn't back down from?"

It was at one of the few frat parties I went to, and yes, it was absolutely the result of a drinking game. She remained one of my friends in San Francisco, though, like the rest, I no longer talk to them. I met Samuel the next month. He was five years older, so that ended the party scene. I had to act mature to prove that my twenty-year-old self was sophisticated enough for a divorced, budding politician.

"Just because you're right doesn't mean I'm not also correct. Cass resents the decision you made and she's taking it out on you."

He shrugs and picks another bite, gaze unfocused as he chews. But I know what he's thinking. Cass's parents' opinions poisoned her and she's infected Ford with them. She doesn't realize that it wasn't just the birth certificate move that forever severed things between them. He wasn't allowed to be there for her from the end of her pregnancy through, basically, now. The scenario paralleled what his birth father did to Maggie, even if Ford tried everything to make it different. No way would Ford risk that situation again. He'd rather be alone than fail another relationship.

"I feel like we should do more than just meet for sex," he says abruptly, yanking me out of my thoughts.

"Wouldn't that be dating?" The idea of dating Ford frightens me as much as it intrigues me. He's sweet, considerate, and caring. Yet I *know* he keeps himself at a distance from women, and why. I've got to tread carefully. To protect both of us.

"No, we'd hang out like friends and not just coworkers. Save the country club BS for our families. What's that thing you do on your days off?"

"Laundry?" I ask wryly and snag the last cheesecake bite. Double chocolate. He saved it for me. "Geocaching."

"Okay. So we go geocaching."

"Geocaching and then back to my place?" I mean it to

be playful, but the reality of what we're planning pumps unbearable heat through my body. Heat that feels like only Ford can release. He's certainly the reason for it.

His gaze grows so intense it steals my breath. "Yeah. That thing, and then back to your place. I guess we can do mine too, since Cass knows about you, but I'm worried she'll come up with an excuse for not dropping Jayden off if she keeps seeing your car there."

One sentence, and my desire cools to arctic temps. Ford continues to cater to that woman's whims, but then, if he didn't, I might've succumbed to Samuel. "No. My place it is. I don't need ex drama."

Am I saying that to agree with him or as a warning to myself?

Nine

Ford

I'm oddly excited to go geocaching with Lia—and nervous. Here I am, fretting over what to fucking wear. As a dude, I've had the luxury of never really worrying about it for a date. Add to that how I never really dated, just going out and hooking up, and this is a new experience.

We aren't going to sit in some bar and flirt for hours before going back to her place. We aren't going to come up with a thousand different titles before we settle on a movie we'd both enjoy. We're going to be active, and I'll break a sweat in a way that I've never done before.

I decide on nicer workout clothes than my regular gym shorts and ratty T-shirt. I'm about to walk out the door a little early for the date when my phone rings.

I answer without looking. "Hello?"

"Ford, Jayden has a doctor's appointment. I need you to meet us there."

My anxiety spikes. "Is there something wrong?"

"Nothing major. I think he has an ear infection."

She mentioned Jayden wasn't feeling good a couple days ago. "What time is the appointment?"

"I'm just pulling into the clinic. It's in ten minutes, but you never know how long we'll end up waiting."

I consider the time. An appointment for an ear infection shouldn't take that long. It's possible I can swing by the clinic, jump into the exam room, and still make it to my date with Lia on time.

"Yeah, I'll be right there."

I squash a beat of irritation. Of all the times for Cass to include me at Jayden's appointment, it's like she has a sixth sense about my date, but there's no way she could know. She called and wants me there. This moment might be a turning point. Twice now, I haven't had to beg to be involved. Lia will understand.

I shoot off a quick message to her about why I might be a little late and jump in the car.

The drive to the clinic only takes minutes. I can't find Cass or Jayden in the waiting room. Stopping at the reception desk, I give them my name. It's only a few seconds before they take me back to an exam room.

Inside, Cass is gently bouncing Jayden on her knee. His cheeks are red and his eyes are glassy. He's not feeling well.

"How's it going?" I ask. Dark circles rim Cass's eyes. Jayden is squirming against her chest.

Her blink is long, like she might fall asleep before she opens her eyes back up. "He's been up fussing all night. I tried Tylenol, ibuprofen, rocking him. We both tried to sleep on the couch. I don't think I've gotten more than three hours of sleep."

I have plenty of sympathy for her, but I'm disappointed. "You could've called."

Her lips thin. "I did."

Yeah, but not until she was overtired and at the doctor's office. I should learn to be grateful for the scraps she throws me. Mom insists that Cass and I should have an equal partnership. I agree. But until I have the means to fight her, I have to take what I can get. Cass's parents won't hesitate to call in favors and block me from seeing my son forever.

Getting angry rarely solves anything. She called me for help and I'll work with that.

I resist looking at my watch. I want to step out and try Lia again, but knowing my luck, that's when the doctor will come in. I sink into the chair next to her and hold my hands out, hoping Jayden will want to come to me. He shrinks into Cass's arms, looking at me like I'm the reason for his discomfort.

He's just a kid, but I have to play nice with his mother so I can become a dad he turns to when he's in pain. Cass shoots me a sincerely apologetic look, and it's one of those rare moments that lowers the wall she's built between us.

The door opens and an older woman walks in. Her pristine lab coat reads *Dr. Prashant*.

She smiles warmly at Cass, her eyes brimming with understanding. "Tell me what's been going on."

Cass gives her the same description she gave me when I walked in. The doctor nods and pins me with a hard look. "You need to let Mom get some rest. There's no rule book that says moms are the only ones with the genetic ability to stay up at night with their kids."

Shock plasters my lips shut. I've dealt with a lot of doctors with attitudes, but none have caught me off guard quite like her. I'd love to be part of Jayden's days and nights. But the fact is that I can only parent as much as she lets me.

Cass stiffens next to me, having the grace to appear chagrined. Yet she doesn't jump to my defense and explain that I'm damn lucky to even be here. She also doesn't tell

Dr. Prashant that her parents are world-renowned pediatric surgeons and can afford an army of attorneys when I can't afford even one, giving her one hundred percent of the parenting power.

I keep my expression unreadable. I don't want to add more bricks to the wall that finally weakened only a couple minutes ago. My situation isn't one that'll change overnight.

Dr. Prashant rattles off instructions for the prescription she hands out. She doesn't spare me one more look but dotes on Cass. I concentrate on what the doctor's saying, not how she's acting, and ignore my simmering resentment. She ushers us out the door and neither Cass nor I say anything as we walk down the long hallway toward the exit.

As we step outside into the warm sun and quiet parking lot, she sighs. "The doctor's right. I need to rest. Do you want to take Jayden for a few hours while I go home and sleep? I can drop him off after I fill his prescription and give him his first dose."

"Absolutely," I say before considering the repercussions. Her request doesn't wipe out the incident in the doctor's office, but it's another olive branch. I can't miss this opportunity just to go on a date. "Why don't I follow you to CVS? I can wait with Jayden and take him home from there."

She considers it for a moment. Her fatigue wins. "Yeah. That'll be good." Her smile is wan. "Thank you, Ford."

"I'm happy to help." The more I'm here for Jayden when Cass needs me to be, the more she'll be on my side. I know I hurt her with my decisions and she retaliated in a way that many consider unforgivable, but I can't change the past.

On the way to the pharmacy, I try Lia again. She answers.

"Hey, did you get my message?" I rub the back of my neck like that'll help the simmering tension dissipate. No way Cass would let me get away with something like this. She used to give me so much shit when I canceled plans to study for a big test in medical school.

"Yes, sorry. I meant to send a reply but got busy going over coordinates. Going a little later will be no problem. I'm ready when you are."

Dammit. She's the one who had to do all the planning for this. And, of course, she's being cool about it. She's Lia, and I still have to cancel on her. "So, Cass hardly got any sleep last night. She asked if I could watch Jayden for a few hours this afternoon. I'm sorry, but I can't make it."

"Oh no, it's no problem." Her voice is steady, but there's more than a hint of disappointment. "I totally understand. He comes first."

I don't want to give up the entire day with Leah. Cass only asked for a few hours. I doubt she'll leave him with me much longer. "You want to come over later tonight?"

More silence. "Are you...are you sure?"

Right. The friends-with-benefits thing. I'm not asking for the benefits now. I want her company because I was looking forward to our date.

"We could catch a movie or something," I offer instead, so she doesn't think I'm inviting her over to get laid. I looked forward to geocaching. It was new and unusual. But now the standard movie date sounds even better. Whatever can keep me from canceling on Lia.

"We don't exactly have the same taste in movies," she says wryly.

No, we don't. I like classics and she likes superhero action movies. Which I like too, only in the movie theater. My screen at home doesn't do them justice.

"I can compromise."

She chuckles. "All right. Why don't you message me when Cass picks him up? I should be back by then."

"You're going out anyway?" It's my turn to be disappointed, but Lia isn't the type to stay at home and wait. She might've been with Samuel, but not with me. I respect her for it. At the same time, I dislike Samuel even more.

"Might as well. This is probably what I would've been doing anyway," she says lightly. She might feel the same way I do about the date, but she's getting on with her life *on her terms*. Unlike Cass, Lia won't anchor herself to a guy and try to destroy his life to make a point.

She'll just leave.

The thought lines my gut with anxiety. My life is rooted here. My job is here. I could be a paramedic anywhere, but Fargo EMS gave me a position as soon as I stepped foot in town again and said I needed a job. I can't ignore that kind of loyalty. Mom is here, and Cass followed me here, and by some miracle, she stayed after our breakup, claiming it was a better place to raise a kid than LA. Whatever happened between us, whatever she's done to me with regards to our son, she's here. I won't leave again.

Lia has no one here but herself. She can go anywhere in the world.

I need to remember that before fate strikes with brutal irony and I'm the one left wanting more.

∩∩

Lia

If I look at my phone one more time, I'm going to throw it off the edge of this trail.

I'm hiking back toward my car, my trail shoes crunching in the dirt. I found my cache hidden on the outer edges of one of a local vineyard and logged my information, but despite the brilliant green views of grapevines as far as the eye can see, nothing about this afternoon has been exactly fun.

By the time I get back to the car and land in a sweaty heap behind the wheel, my phone is still silent. I double-check the reception, which was spotty on the trail, but I have all my bars.

I check the time. Four hours have passed since Ford called.

I take my time hiking, then meander over the trail through the vineyards. I spent even more time perusing all the other call signs written in the cache's logbook and tried to guess the story behind all the trading objects they'd left behind.

My trading object is bandages. Fun ones. My call sign is Emergency Girl. Today, I left behind an emoji bandage and the souvenir I took was a simple mood ring. According to the ring, I'm feeling warm and loving, but I think the summer sun has more to do with the color change. I doubt there's a ring color for feeling let down.

Ford said a couple of hours, but it's clearly taking longer. My brain wants to revert to the helplessness of hanging around an empty house for Samuel when he was working late. The damn thing won't stop conjuring old emotions. Like anger when I realized he might not have been working, that his fling with his ex-wife wasn't a one-time mistake.

To combat the surge of my past, I refuse to linger by my phone and do nothing tonight. I run through a list of movies I could watch by myself when I get home. What's something fun I can do for dinner? Pizza and movie night? Ice cream and movie night? No, that resembles too many days post-Samuel-breakup. Pizza and a movie it is.

By the time I arrive home, I decide to make my own

after I shower. I take my time in the bathroom, luxuriating in the steam and my vanilla body wash because nothing else pleasurable is happening tonight.

In the kitchen, I set my phone on the counter. It dings as soon as it drops out of my hand. Scrambling to pick it up, I prop my elbows on the countertop and peer at the message.

She still hasn't come to pick up Jayden. Sorry.

Disappointment curls in my gut. I'd offer to help, but this is Ford's bonding time with his son. It's his chance to show Cass that a good father does more than make a lot of money.

No problem. Hope he's feeling better. And I really do. My day didn't turn out as planned, but neither did theirs.

Feeling moderately better, I rummage through the cupboards, gathering all the ingredients I need for a greasy, cheesy pizza.

My phone rings. Ford.

My arms are loaded, but to keep from being that pathetic girl who hangs on every call waiting for her man, I take my time arranging them on the counter before answering. "Hello?"

"This wasn't supposed to be how today went," Ford says in a low voice.

"Is he sleeping?"

"After three hours of fussing, yes. No wonder Cass was so tired. It's the only reason I haven't called her yet."

"Not the only reason. You're still enjoying your time with him."

"Yeah," he says softly. "I really am. I've never gotten to experience this part of fatherhood before. I almost feel guilty. He's miserable, but I'm wandering around the house with a dopey smile on my face."

"I'm really glad you were able to help." I'm also glad I

didn't sit at home, but I wish I could've done more than offer supportive messages.

"I wish we could've gone on the date, too."

"We'll have another chance. I'm just gonna make myself a pizza and find the most explosive action movie I can." I keep my voice chipper. Ford needs support, not to feel like crap because he had to cancel.

"The way you watch those shows, I'm surprised you didn't become a cop instead of a paramedic."

"Less paperwork."

"Agreed." There's a beat of silence where neither of us knows what else to say. We could talk for hours during the slow points of our shifts, but this whole kinda-sorta dating thing is new territory. "I better let you go."

"Take care. And seriously, don't worry about today. See you at work on Monday?" Sundays don't really seem like a date day, so I don't bring up getting together tomorrow. I'm sure we're both thinking that tomorrow was supposed to have been spent lounging in bed together after a late night, most definitely *not* sleeping.

"See you Monday." He sounds as disappointed as I feel.

I busy myself with supper. Once my pizza's ready and my house smells like tomato sauce, I settle on the couch and select a movie. I hit start on an old-time action flick that I've seen no less than ten times. I guess tonight is about comfort food, comfortable pajamas, and comforting entertainment.

The movie wraps up and my empty plate is abandoned on the coffee table. Do I watch another movie and stay up late for an entirely different reason than originally planned?

My doorbell rings. It's already dark out. Who would be stopping by this late? In San Francisco, I had an active social life that included parties I didn't care to go to, Samuel's luncheons, and my family's fundraisers. But here in Fargo, my social life doesn't exist.

I creep to my front door and peek out the peephole.

On the other side of the circle of warped glass is Ford, hands stuffed in his jeans pockets, hair all rumpled like he's run his hands through it a million times.

I'm in pajama boxer shorts and my cami. Not exactly presentable, but at least I don't have pizza stains on my top.

It's Ford. It shouldn't matter if I'm in my uniform or my pajamas. But it does.

My house is dark. I could pretend I'm asleep. Maybe he didn't see the TV flickering. Maybe he didn't see me moving around. It's Ford. He drove across town at night and he's here. So, do I open the door and invite him in?

Ten

Ford

Fuck, this is a bad idea. She's probably not even going to answer. What single woman, sitting home alone, is going to whip open their door after dark?

I should've called. Should've messaged. But by the time Cass left after stumbling through my house, collecting Jayden's things and apologizing profusely for how long she'd napped, I didn't even realize I'd made this decision.

When Cass drove off, I was in my car and parked outside of Lia's home before I knew it.

There's no going back. I ring the doorbell. Either she'll answer, or she won't.

The door inches open. She's scrubbed clean of all makeup, and her hair's tumbling over her shoulders like it's had little more than a finger comb. She's disheveled and sexy as hell.

"Is everything all right?" she asks.

Her rich voice is enough to short-circuit my mind,

which is already struggling with her take-me-to-bed appeal. I nudge the door open farther. She steps back, her confused gaze on me, her brow wrinkling.

"I had to come," is all I say. I take another second to drink her in. The frilly shorts she's wearing bare her legs more than anything I've seen her wear. Her skimpy shirt fails to conceal her full breasts.

Damn, she has nice tits. Creamy and round, I can fondle them while I suck a sweet nipple into my mouth.

Lust rams into me. I've admired every other part of her body, including her brain, but this is the most I've seen of parts I've been trying hard not to think about for over a year. Now, they're right here, and the reasons why I shouldn't do this aren't coming to mind. Instead, the memory of her sultry voice saying, "We're adults," loops over and over in my head, drilling need into me until I have to taste Lia more than I have to breathe. Desire coils under my skin, writhing, waiting for a sign from her, anything that says it's okay for me to unleash everything I'm holding back.

Way too long passes before I lift my gaze to her face. Even in the dark, it's obvious her cheeks are flushed. Probably because she can tell I want to eat her alive.

"You're here," she breathes. "Now what?"

I back her into the wall. It's not like me to be the aggressor. I usually don't have to be. I'm not exactly fighting them off, but I also don't have to prove how fucking much I want this. "What do two adults usually do when they're alone together?" I lean back just enough to rake my gaze down her long body. "Especially when one of those adults is wearing pretty pink pajamas that show me *everything*."

Lia's lips part and her eyes flare, but she doesn't shrink away. We're moving at light speed, blurring the lines. One of us should point that out, but it's not like either of us has been in this situation before. People might assume I have all the experience, but with Lia, I'm a rookie all over again.

She licks her lips and rests her hot hands on my shoulders. As soon as she touches me, my body ignites. My muscles shake with the effort to restrain myself. Real relationship or not, Lia means something to me. The best thing to do would be to turn on my heel and leave.

The only thing that could peel me off Lia is Lia herself.

I lower my head until my lips are a whisper above hers. "Do you want this?"

Her breath hitches. "It seems like the best idea and the worst idea at the same time."

"Exactly." I close the distance. My mouth lands on hers, and like the other times we've kissed, I'm lost. She's solid, she's real. She's not the coworker I'm forbidden to have dirty thoughts about. She's not a random hookup I have to keep at an emotional distance. She's my partner, my friend. She's also undeniably sexy and now she's mine.

I should get an award for my restraint this past year.

But the dam's been blown. All the things I want to do to this woman are flooding my brain.

A hint of pizza lingers on her lips. I blame it on my skipped dinner, but I want to devour her. Sweeping in, I dive deeper, plastering her back against the wall. She wraps her arms around me and I lift her up by her ass cheeks. There's nothing I want more right now than her legs anchored around my waist, except for our clothes to magically disappear.

She hesitates, her toes still touching the ground. Ripping her mouth away, she says, "I can't. I'm too big."

"I don't know who the fuck ever told you that," I growled, "but it's a lie. Wrap your legs around me and tell me where your bedroom is before I fuck you against the wall." Hooking my fingers around her waistband, I yank down. "That's actually a good idea."

I lower her shorts all the way, dropping to my knees with them.

"Ford, I...my bedroom."

"Here works just fine." Judging from her excited but scandalized expression, someone has been giving this magnificent woman boring-as-hell sex. She's probably experienced little more than two positions—missionary and on top. Maybe he gave it to her from behind once in a while to be wild.

I hitch one of her legs over my shoulder and meet her gaze. She's open to me, but I want to see her reaction.

Her lips are parted and her hands are glued to the wall. The anticipation is clear in her eyes—she wants to know what I'm going to do next.

I delight in showing her.

I part her slick folds with my thumbs and look into her eyes. "You're wet for me."

A slight nod. My lips tilt in a smile before I sink in.

She's hot and wet and so responsive, her hips kicking out as soon as my tongue flicks her clit.

I lick across her folds and enjoy the tremble in her legs. I tease her with short, fast licks, then draw them out, lightly sucking after a few strokes. Her moans grow louder and she anchors her hands in my hair to ride my face. I hope Mrs. Rosenthal is a deep sleeper because I'm going to make Lia scream.

I lighten the strokes and test her entrance with a finger. So fucking tight, like the rest of her. Muscles flex in her legs as she undulates against me. Slowly, I push my finger in and her body tightens around me. Her hands tangle harder in my hair.

For most of my life, sex has been a means to an end. Get

her off, get me off. But this is an exploration. I missed exploring the vineyards with her earlier. I won't miss this.

In and out, I alternate my tongue with my finger. She's riding the edge, her moans and gasps filling the dark room. When I can't stand it anymore, when I have to be inside her, I flick my tongue in circles. Her body tenses and she bends her leg higher.

"Oh God, *Ford*."

Heat explodes across my face as she cries my name even louder. She bucks against me, but I hold her up. The moment she passes her peak, I rise, shoving my pants down. My cock springs free, straining for her.

Her eyes are half-lidded and she's breathing hard. Satisfaction rips through me. I lift the same leg that was on my shoulder and put it around my waist. The tip of my dick touches hot, wet paradise and I jerk like someone's whacked me with the cardiac paddles.

Lia gasps the same thing I'm thinking. "Protection."

I yank my hips away from her and the heaven I just tasted. "Shit. Sorry."

I've only been that careless once. Cass's birth control wasn't enough then, and I've never gone without since. It takes me seconds to retrieve the condom from my wallet, rip it open, and roll it on. The entire time, I have her pinned against the wall, waiting.

This time, when I lift her legs, she doesn't resist. She's propped against me like she was born to fuck me against the wall. I capture her mouth as I push inside. Once I'm fully seated, I take a moment to breathe through the staggering bliss crashing through me. She makes the first move with a roll of her hips.

Fuck. "You're going to kill me," I murmur against her lips.

"I've already died," she whispers, and that's the last talking we do.

I pull out and thrust in and repeat, a mindless, rutting beast. Her walls grip me and my pleasure wipes out coherent thought.

I can't get enough of her. I clamp my hands on her hips. I kiss along her cheek and down her neck and nibble at the base of her throat. She's writhing against me and she might climax again if I have enough control to slow the hell down. I don't.

Electricity gathers at the base of my spine and my balls tighten a second before my orgasm slams into me.

If I didn't have a mouth full of her, I might make more of a racket than she did.

She flexes and spasms around me as I release so hard, so deep inside of her, I'm worried the latex won't hold. Any concern was obliterated when she came again.

We breathe into each other. She's trapped between me and the wall, but I'm not sure who's holding who up.

Usually, at this point, I'd say something cocky or drop some comment to make it clear where we're going from here —no cuddles, no breakfast.

Not this time. I need a few moments to recover.

She tilts her face against mine. "Is everything okay?"

I study her. "Amazing. You?"

Her lips quirk with a hint of shyness that goes straight to my heart. "I guess I'm doing okay."

I chuckle and tighten my hold around her. We're both still wearing our shirts. There's so much of her I haven't seen yet.

"So...where's your bedroom?"

∩∩

Lia

Water sluices off my body as I kneel in the shower. Ford towers over me, his expression as earnest as a kid getting his first brand-new bike.

I stroke my hand along his length. He's really big. Long and thick, he fills every part of me.

How can this man make me feel so feminine and dainty? It's not like this at work. On our shifts, we're equals. He doesn't cater to me and he expects me to hold up my end of the job.

Here, in my place? He *carried* me to the bedroom. I'm nearly six feet tall and not at all willowy and he walked like I was nothing more than a fanny pack. A mostly naked one. And he worshiped me all night long.

I lost count of how many orgasms he gave me, and by morning, we ran out of condoms, creating the perfect opportunity for me to go down on him for once.

I take him into my mouth. I've never been big into blowing a guy, so it's pleasantly surprising that I actually want to. I want to do this for Ford, and I want to experience him as fully as he experienced me.

This strong, unflappable man is coming apart in my shower because of me. His body is shaking. He's propped his arms on the shower wall and he's trembling, moaning my name over and over.

I don't know how much time has passed. I'm usually counting down the seconds, rushing the job so I can be done, but I'm absorbed in how he tastes, how he clenches when I swirl my tongue, and I love prolonging his pleasure.

"I'm gonna come," he gasps. "If you don't want to... Lia!" He groans and rolls his head back.

Usually, I'm not a swallower. The thought would make

me dry heave. Ford's different there too. I want him. I want to taste all of him.

He goes rigid and heat explodes in my mouth. I hang on to his hip with one hand as he shakes and moans my name. I never get tired of hearing him say it. I've been Wescott to him for so long that when he calls me Lia, it's more intimate. He's let down his guard around me. Wescott kept me in the coworker category. We were buddies. When he calls me Lia, we're more. It doesn't matter that plenty of other people call me that too. Not Ford. He's too careful. We could be friends with benefits and he would still call me Wescott, but he hasn't.

I sit back on my heels and grin up at him. His flagging erection bobs in my face. The wondrous way he gazes at me makes me feel special. Cherished.

I can almost forget this isn't real.

I rise to cover the sting that thought gives me.

He helps me up, his hands cupping my elbows.

"I don't know where you learned how to do that, but I'm grateful."

"Presley's School for the Gifted Blow Jobber?"

He chuckles as he folds me in his embrace and moves us both under the spray. My water bill is going to be atrocious.

He rinses us both off, his movements unhurried and soft. "What'd you have planned for today?"

"Housecleaning, but I might be too worn out for that."

"Want to grab some food?"

"I'd like that."

Excitement wells in my belly before I force it back down. This isn't a date.

No date has ever rocked my world like this.

"Food," he says and turns the faucet off. He gives me a knowing look, water dripping down his face. "Then I've gotta get more condoms."

Eleven

Ford

It's just a lunch date.

That's what I keep telling myself as we grab some sandwiches. But I'm having way more fun than I normally do getting a fucking sandwich.

She's thrown her hair up into a messy bun and she's wearing a simple purple top with jean shorts. One time, she told me she loves wearing whatever she wants to now and not worrying about what'll impress people or what colors go best with her skin on camera. Her pink lips wrap around a metal straw as she takes a pull from her lemonade. It brings me straight back to this morning in the shower.

Coming in her mouth is an unparalleled experience. Unless I count every other time with her.

Why is she different? Is it the friends and no expectations thing? I'm not around anyone who doesn't expect something from me. I get it. That's life. Only Mom and Lia expect me to be just me, without a fat paycheck and initials behind my name to define me.

"Don't you have plans to help your mom today?"

I rip my gaze off her mouth. She's eyeing her sandwich. Good. My lewd thoughts are probably etched all over my face. "She usually calls by Friday and she didn't."

"Maybe she's worried about interfering with any plans we might have. You should call her."

My mind takes a beat to register her request. I was so ready for something along the lines of *Good, you're a grown man. Your mom can take care of herself.* Not encouragement to call her.

Cass resented Mom more each year we were together. *She's too dependent on you.* Cass doesn't understand that Mom's not relying on me. I just want to help her and be around for her. She has no one else.

"I'll give her a call later."

She lifts a shoulder. "You can do it now. I don't mind."

"You don't?"

Her incredulous look says enough, but she still speaks around her bite of sandwich. "Why would I?"

"We're hanging out."

"I can help her out, too. Seriously, I don't mind. Sundays off work are pretty mellow." She takes a bite, crunching through her sandwich. She offered to help Mom *just like that.*

I don't sense any hidden agenda. Because it's Lia and she likes my mom and she likes lending a hand. Last month, she helped Mitch's wife hang curtains because Mitch worked the weekend.

That's what friends do.

She leaves her food alone and studies me. "Unless you don't want to fool your mom any more than we need to."

That's my out. As much as I like her offer, that's the

problem. I like it too much. We're sleeping together. Mom likes her and the feeling's mutual. This could get too jumbled in my brain.

Yet the words to turn her down aren't forming on my tongue.

My phone vibrates with a message.

Can you take Jayden again this afternoon?

I'm saved for a moment. "Excuse me for a sec."

Lia waves me off and keeps eating.

I don't leave the table, but I push my tray a little farther away. Of course I want to take Jayden again. I haven't called Mom yet. Unless...

Can I take him with me to Mom's?

I hold my breath, waiting for her reply. Restricting Mom's visits with Jayden has always been a major control point for Cass, a way to punctuate how betrayed she felt when I put Mom's needs before our relationship.

Her message is quicker than I expected. *That's fine. Can you pick him up?*

What made Cass turn this corner? Whether it's single motherhood or that she thinks I've cleaned up my game, I don't care at the moment. I finally get to not only have my son, but my mom gets to be a grandma. I grin up at Lia. "Do you mind if Jayden's with us?"

"You get him *again*?" She sits back, stunned. "And she's letting you take him to your mom's?"

"If it's okay with you."

"Why wouldn't it be?"

"I bailed on you last night."

"For good reason." Her gaze sharpens. "Do you want your own time with him? I don't want to interfere with your mom's afternoon. I know it doesn't happen often."

Weathering other women with my son is a new experience. Even if Cass hadn't played her custody games with me,

I would've been cautious about who I let around my kid and who he got attached to. I didn't think twice about Lia being around him. She's the furthest thing from a bad influence. Yet she hasn't claimed to want to stay in Fargo or even in North Dakota.

Last night and this morning is starting to look more like a mistake than expected.

No. This is the line I'm not crossing. To everyone else, we're dating, but no matter how mind-blowing sex with her is, Lia has made it clear in the past that her sojourn in Fargo is just a stop on the way to something else. I will stay here and do what I need to do. And I need to stay on my side of the line to keep our situation from getting complicated.

So why is the first thing out of my lips an invitation for more?

"Join us. You won't interfere with me and Mom. Besides, I think there's a reason Cass is suddenly so willing to share parental duties, and it started when I told her we were dating. You'll only help me get more time with Jayden." Yes, Jayden. That's why we're doing this. I need to keep reminding myself of the reason we agreed to pretend to date in the first place.

She pauses with a chip halfway to her mouth, then rests it on her plate. "I'm happy for you, and of course I'd love to hang out with Jayden and Maggie. But Ford, we shouldn't need to do this to get Cass to act like a decent human being."

"If it's what I gotta do, I don't mind."

"You still need a long-term plan."

We've had this conversation before. The longer I wait to fight for custody, the harder it's going to be. I'm finally getting on top of student loans and Mom's finances are stable, but it's still going to be a while before I can afford a lawyer. "A long-term plan will be easier if my son knows who I am and is comfortable around me."

Sympathy lights her eyes. "I know. I'm sorry. Count this as the only moment I regret not going to law school. I wouldn't have gone into family law, but I could've helped you out."

She's mentioned that before. "How would Samuel have handled you going to law school and not being at his beck and call?"

She wrinkles her nose. "He's a big-picture guy. It's why he divorced his first wife. She was a career woman through and through and he wanted to be the guy on stage, with a wife and two-point-two children by his side while he was sworn into office. She wasn't willing to commit to that yet in her twenties."

I couldn't picture Lia ready to commit to it either. Samuel must've thought otherwise. Or he'd gotten to her early enough to groom her into the perfect package. "How would you wave while holding your two-point-two children as he got sworn into office?"

Without hesitating, she flashes a superficial grin straight out of a Hollywood magazine and waves her hand, a dainty move that'd make Miss America take notes. The move is experienced. She's done it before, just without the husband and kids.

Her expression changes to a scowl. "He thought he was helping me subvert my parents with the whole law school thing. Except he was just doing what they did and corralling me into what he wanted me to do."

"So instead of being a high-powered lawyer with top political connections, a big house, and perfect children, you're okay hanging out with me and Jayden?"

"Add in saving lives on the side, and I'm fine for now."

The *for now* lingers between us as we finish our meal.

Lia

"Can you stay for supper?" Maggie sways on the edge of her first-story deck, Jayden on her hip. His fine, dusty hair's all mussed from a nap. He's cuddled against Maggie's shoulder, all pink cheeks and glassy eyes.

It took all of five minutes for him to warm up to his grandma and they've been inseparable ever since. Maggie stayed inside to keep an ear out for Jayden while Ford and I did yard work. When Ford moved his mom to this small, easily maintainable apartment, Maggie was given a deal on her rent in exchange for some light cleaning and maintenance around the building. Behind each side-by-side apartment, a small strip of grass separates the deck from the gate to the patio area that she's charged with. The property managers hire yard workers to get everything going when the seasons change, while Maggie takes care of weeds and tends to the flower beds between visits.

The pool and party house that are part of the apartment complex are partly her responsibility too. She tests the water each day and does the daily cleaning. A service will come in for anything more. It's gone a long way toward whittling down the debt his stepdad left.

Ford straightens from the rock-filled flower bed he's weeding and wipes his brow. "Are you okay with that?"

As if I have other plans on a Sunday night. Even if I did, I'd rather be here. "That's fine."

I'm enjoying my time. So far, I haven't gotten to visit with Maggie much. She's been in full grandma mode, and that's been its own joy to watch. She was on the floor, crawling around with her grandson. Ford brought an old

Fargo EMS tote bag full of toys over and a pair of tiny swimming trunks.

I expected stuffed animals or something, but there was only one. Half the toys make noise and hold Jayden's interest for maybe five minutes. Then there are the building blocks, both the Duplos and some plain wooden ones with letters and shapes etched into them. Jayden gnaws on them both.

Ford takes his work gloves off and nimbly steps out of the rocks to the grass. "Hey, Mom, mind if we take Jayden in the pool before supper's ready?"

"Not at all. I'll get him ready while you change."

I look down at my dusty shorts. I haven't sweated through my T-shirt material, so I'm still presentable, but I didn't bring a swimsuit.

Humor mixes with suggestion. "You can strip down to your bra and underwear."

"That will go over well if Cass finds out."

He chuckles and picks up the bucket of weeds we pulled. "I'll be in the water with him and we're staying in the shallow end."

"I can sit on the edge."

Ford disappears into the tool shed on the other side of the pool house and cleans up everything while I swat the dust off me, then go inside to wash up.

When I'm done, I check with Maggie in the kitchen. "Do you need help with anything?"

She's showing Jayden all the different ingredients she's going to use for the meal. She leaves him with a colander and a wooden spoon and crosses to me. "Not at all. You're going swimming?"

"They are." I point to my clothes. "I'll spectate."

"I'm so glad you could come today."

The happiness in her eyes drags on the blanket of deception I'm hiding under. I'm lying to this wonderful woman. I was never nervous around Maggie the few times I met her before, but her delighted expression makes me want to run.

I default to the deflection-by-flattery tactics I used for talking with my mom's donors. "Thanks for having me over. Whatever you're making, it looks like it'll be delicious."

She glances at the fresh vegetables piled next to the box of pasta. "Don't those tomatoes look too good to eat? I think they call them heirloom tomatoes, but they were too pretty not to buy." She sighs wistfully. "It's so nice to be able to splurge every now and then."

I'm glad Maggie reached the *buy farmers' market tomatoes* level of splurging, but that's not a huge impulse purchase.

"I also bought the lettuce there, too. They were actually cheaper than the supermarket, and I bet each leaf has so much more flavor."

My parents used to have the best produce delivered on grocery days. Our housekeeper would accept the delivery and put the load away. I heard her once when I was a teenager muttering about how much better the one percent eat.

I didn't know at the time what the one percent was. Living on my own, making my own meager wage, I get that now. Just like I get Maggie's thrill at being able to buy locally and pay a little more for quality.

The first month I lived on my own and enrolled in the EMT program, I blew a large chunk of savings. A new, if plainer wardrobe, sparse furniture, and the EMT course—it wasn't cheap. I was coming off a job that paid well and I no longer had incoming money or someone to share expenses with. Of course, my fiancé both shared our living expenses and employed me, which made lining up my own career that much more important.

I'm finally building savings again. The thought of *What next?* has popped up more than once. I've never had an answer.

What next?

I love Mrs. Rosenthal, but she's not going to be around forever. The next landlord is going to charge a higher rent. Without Mrs. Rosenthal, I'll probably want to move rather than live right on top of another family.

I could move.

I blink at the realization. I could move *now*.

"Go on out." Maggie waves me out of the kitchen. "Have fun. I've got supper taken care of."

My feet move, but my mind stays on thoughts of leaving Fargo. I came here to start over. Now, I have a versatile career. I have work experience. I don't have debt.

Where would I go?

I stop before the entrance and stare through the glass at the blue of the pool. The door slides open behind me and Ford's voice is a welcome distraction. "I'll be right back."

I nod without looking back and go inside. The pool house is empty. Kicking off my sandals, I sit on the edge of the water by the entry stairs. My gaze lingers on the water as if some chlorine mermaid will rise and tell me my future.

Going back to San Francisco isn't an option. I furrow my brow. It's not because of Samuel.

I can picture his dark eyes, his perfectly combed hair with the manageable cowlick on the right side. The way he used to look at me, how he used to be so sweet, I'd forget everything. I'd forget that I hated the hustle and bustle of campaigning. I'd forget how much it sucked to think about what I looked like every single time I left the house. I'd forget that I wasn't ready to settle down and have my life revolve around someone else.

I can remember his sweet words and his low, sexy voice and I don't want it. I don't want him.

Going back to California isn't an option because of the cost, not because I'm afraid I'll fall harder for Samuel than I did before.

I blow out a breath. Whoa.

My feet swing in the cool water. I'm free. For the first time since I left home, I'm free to do whatever the hell I want, wherever the hell I want.

The entrance door bangs open.

"How's the water?" Ford's in plain black trunks and his defined chest is hidden by a toddler in matching trunks and a white-and-black-striped swim shirt. Jayden squirms to get down as soon as they're close to the steps, a rubber ducky clutched in his tiny hands. "Hold on, big guy."

"The water's great, but it looks like you're going to earn every bit of your lifeguard training with that one."

"Right?" He spins Jayden around in his arms and descends into the water. Jayden giggles and kicks his feet as soon as the water touches them. "Between coaching and life-guarding, you'd think I trained for this dad gig my entire life."

"Don't forget the pediatrician part."

Muscles ripple across his back, but his gaze stays on Jayden as he splashes and giggles. "I didn't do the pediatrician part."

"I don't mean to pry…" I don't, but I've learned to tread carefully around this subject. "Have you thought of another type of residency, like family medicine or emergency? It's not too late, not for someone with your caliber of training and experience."

"Except that most other medical students have my caliber of training and experience and they didn't give up when life got tough."

"Neither did you."

The look he gives me says I should know better. "The residency programs won't see it like that. Besides, I can't take the risk I'll get accepted into a position in a different town."

The finality in his voice should stop more questions, but I have one more. "What if Cass moves?"

"She won't." He helps Jayden onto the top stair, where he can sit and play with the water going to his belly. Ford sits a couple of steps down, the water lapping his strong chest. "She's got a good job in hospital administration and she's out from under her parents' thumb." He cocks a brow. "Sound familiar?"

Other than the job part, where I'm making much less each year. "I can go at any time, Ford. There's nothing keeping her in town but you."

He frowns. "There's Jayden."

The boy glances up at his name and grins. Ford bobs the rubber duck and Jayden squeals and makes a grab for it.

"She's here for you. With her family's money, she could go anywhere. She wants you." I wait for the insecure jealousy that usually haunts me when I think of Samuel's ex-wife, but instead, I'm just worried for Ford.

He looks at me and sees how serious I am. His gaze goes back to Jayden. "Say you're right about *Becky*." He waits to make sure I get it. Jayden might not be able to tell his mom what we're saying, but we're not sure what he can understand.

"Okay. About Becky?"

"Right. Why would Becky want her friend to settle down if she was waiting for him to do that with her?"

"Because she's still in love with him." His mouth flattens. He doesn't believe me. "At least her idea of him, of who he was supposed to be when they were together."

"I don't see it."

"You might not, but when Becky does, she might realize that nothing else ties her here. Not a potential husband, not a custody agreement, nothing."

Ford rescues the yellow duck from floating too far. "Becky was the one that ended things."

"She might regret it. What if it was a manipulative move that didn't work? You have—Becky's friend has his whole life in front of him. He needs to figure out a way to keep what's really important to him."

"Becky's friend needs more money," he says tightly.

And we're back to the beginning. Every time we've talked about his issues with Cass, we go in the same circle. Pretty soon, that circle's going to shrink until it's just a noose around his neck.

∩∩

Ford

As Jayden's bedtime creeps closer, I know I have to get him home, but Mom brought out the picture albums. She's got Jayden on her lap at the kitchen table. The album is spread open in front of Lia and I'm on the other side.

Lia points to the trophy held up by a bunch of five-year-old boys. "You didn't tell me the team you coached took first."

"They didn't. That's an adult league trophy, but I told them to do that for the picture."

She laughs. An open, generous sound. This is nothing like going through these pictures with Cass. First of all, Cass had to be almost bolted to the chair to look at the photos. Then all she focused on was the fashion of the time, like

Mom's "Rachel cut" and the eighties car Mom drove in the nineties.

"Oh, these are going backward in time. Oh well." Mom nudges Lia to open a new album.

Lia smiles over my senior pictures and asks about the experience, not the style of clothing I'm wearing. She giggles over the shots of me at the Fargo Zoo when I was fourteen, then the time when I was twelve and got my one and only Mom haircut.

"That was unfortunate," Mom says between laughs. "Every time I grabbed a pair of scissors for years after that, he ran."

Lia points to a picture of three scrawny kids, dripping wet, with popsicles in their hands. "Look at Ryan and Karoline. That's a nice picture of all of you."

"I know you don't remember them, but there were happy times," Mom says quietly.

Like the day that picture was taken. Mom set up the sprinklers and we played for hours. She showered us with snacks and sunscreen, and we watched movies all night, falling asleep on the floor.

Yeah. There were some happy times. A beat of longing goes through me. I wasn't an only child those years after Mom married, but I look back on that time like I was.

Lia opens a new album, this one full of photos of me around Jayden's age. "Aww, look how much you look alike."

Pride swells in me. Jayden has my hair color and gets his eye color from Cass. But his cheeky grin is all mine.

I reach over and point out the baby photos to a sleepy Jayden. He's about to pass out against Mom's chest. "We should go before he falls asleep and then stays awake all night on Cass."

"There's only one album left," Mom says, and Lia sets the old one down, picking up the new one.

"How much older can we get than when I was a baby?"

Mom chuckles and shifts Jayden to the other knee. He leans over the table to grab at the pages. "No, honey," Mom whispers and twists her body so he can't reach. "I found this one when I was cleaning boxes out the other day."

Lia flips a page. There's Mom with my grandparents. She doesn't talk about them much. Other than getting a Christmas card every year, I don't talk to them either. Another page and there's a picture of Mom hugging a familiar man.

My stomach drops. My dad. He's grinning, his arm possessively around Mom's waist. He's leaning against a red Mustang, wearing black slacks and a white business shirt.

"That's a nice car. Did you drive it?" Lia asks Mom.

"No. That was Nathaniel's. Ford's dad." Before uncomfortable silence can descend over the room, Mom adds with a chuckle, "You can guess where he got his name."

Lia snickers. "Oh my God, you never told me."

The dark moment is lost on Mom and Lia. There he is, my birth father, hugging my mom like she means something. And Mom named me Ford as if that'd bring my dad back into her life. She must've waited for him so long, hoping the entire time.

Is that what Lia thinks Cass is doing? Waiting for me? Does that mean that no matter how much I try to be different, to be there for my son, I'm still like Nathaniel?

No, I'm better than that, better than him. I can't force myself to be in love with Cass, but I can stick around and show her that I can be there for our son.

Lia turns the page and there my dad is again. A stethoscope around his neck, wearing a lab coat.

"He was a doctor?" she asks, her incredulous gaze shifting to mine.

"Didn't Ford tell you? Nathanial is a pediatrician in Baltimore."

Lia's gaze doesn't leave mine. "A pediatrician?"

"Johns Hopkins," I say woodenly before pushing back from the table. "If I can't be a better pediatrician than him, at least I'm a better father."

"You're a wonderful father, Ford." Mom kisses the top of Jayden's head. "Grandma's going to miss you."

She hands him off and Lia helps me gather all of his stuff and pack it.

We load Jayden up and when Mom goes back inside, I turn to Lia. "Would you mind driving so I can entertain Jayden and keep him awake for Cass?"

"No problem." She takes the keys and looks back at the house. "Your dad is a pediatrician at a world-renowned children's hospital."

"He was nothing but a sperm donor."

"Seems like he had more influence than that."

My jaw grinds. "He had a shit ton of influence and none of it good."

"You're not your dad, Ford. And you're better than your stepdad ever gave you credit for."

"I know."

"Do you?"

"Of course, Lia. But not all of us are born with the opportunity to go wherever we want and be whatever we want. Some of us are rooted to a spot out of necessity. I'm okay with it. I just wish everyone else was."

I slide into the back seat with Jayden and Lia gets in to drive. Neither of us says much, even after we drop Jayden off.

Twelve

Lia

"You've been quiet." It's my third shift working with Ford this week. He hasn't referred to anything about last weekend.

I can't quit thinking about it.

He pulls out of the hospital bay. Our elderly male patient with the broken hip is in good hands. The nurse we left him with is one of Ford's old conquests and her smile was as shiny as her new engagement ring. Ford usually flashes his trademark grin and indulges in a little flirting—after we've left the patient's room and are navigating our way through the ER. But today, he only gave her a polite nod, then left to restock meds.

"We're working."

"It's more than that. You're upset."

"I'm not." He shifts his gaze toward me and his jaw flexes. "I'm not."

I wave my finger between us. "This isn't us. You haven't

given me shit once for being five minutes late yesterday." I had a flat tire and only one bar on my phone, so I could barely watch YouTube to learn how to change it. I finally had to call a tow truck and a ride.

"So you didn't know how to change a tire. I'm not giving you trouble for that, and you talked to the boss."

"Ford. Out with it."

He drapes a hand over the wheel. "Are we at the nagging stage of our fake relationship?"

I don't know whether to laugh or be offended. "I swear to God, Ford, we can be at the 'you can walk home' stage of our relationship."

"That's parenting, not dating." He goes quiet for a moment as he maneuvers onto the boulevard that'll take us to our station. "Think I should talk to Cass?"

"About custody?"

"No, about whether she's, you know, waiting around for me or something."

I was the one who brought it up. I should have an answer, but I don't. "I wish I knew. I have no idea how she'd take a question like that."

"She might pick up and leave."

"Maybe that was why she gave you an ultimatum. Until you moved on, she couldn't move on, but moving on with you still didn't feel right."

"Maybe." He waves to a patrol car that passes. "I guess we keep playing this out and see where it goes."

He means with regards to Cass, but as soon as he says it, I want to nod emphatically and say yes, let's keep dating and see where it goes. I can't mix fake dating with sleeping together in a relationship that isn't there.

After the weekend we spent together, I'm tempted to tell him I want to see where *we* can go.

"I still owe you a geocache date," he says suddenly.

I'm hung up on the word *date* and the thrill racing down my spine. God, are those butterflies in my belly? I press a hand to my stomach. I haven't been excited about going out with someone in a long time. Probably because I haven't gone out with anyone for forever. Samuel and I were at that comfortable stage in our relationship. Besides living together, our dates were career-focused—*his* career. "I have a hike planned for tomorrow."

"I'm free tomorrow."

So much for keeping my head around Ford, I jump at the chance. "We can go right away in the morning. Want to sleep over?"

"Lia, you're going to make me drive this rig right into traffic. If they have to call 9-1-1 and I get the rookie that still turns green at the sight of blood, I'll never forgive you."

My laugh is cut off by the radio's squelch. "Adult female in respiratory distress at…"

I'm grateful for the interruption only because the rest of the shift will go by quickly. Then, I get to have a sleepover.

♘♘

Ford

"Is this all we're bringing?" I heft the backpack. Only the water bottles make it heavy. Other than that, there are some granola bars, a flashlight, a first aid kit, bug spray, and sunscreen. I'm also carrying the rain gear. Lia's pack has all the same along with a small trowel, what looks like the little mirror my dentist shoves in my mouth, a small magnet, and a pocket knife.

She tosses a logbook and pen into her red backpack.

"That's all we should need. I don't think this one will be hard to find."

"Why the bandages?"

"I leave those behind for swag."

"Swag in a geocache?" I'm so out of my element here. I had the idea that we were hiking. But she's not wearing performance gear and hiking boots. She's got on nothing more than athletic shoes, khaki pants she's rolled to her shins, and a pale-blue T-shirt as if geocaching is nothing more than a walk on a paved path.

I could've asked what I'd need, but I was so damn intent on getting between her thighs that I raced home after work, packed a bag, and popped up on her doorstep. She greeted me with grilled burgers and a couple of beers. Then we compromised on a movie that was neither a blockbuster nor an indie flick before I finally got to taste her again.

When she came on my tongue the first time, I didn't care about what had happened last weekend, not anymore. The doubts that had stayed with me, not just about Cass but about what Lia had said about my dad, had robbed me of enough sleep. I got better shut-eye last night than I did all week.

"Ready?" she asks.

"Lead the way."

She drives, getting on the interstate and taking us farther out of town than I expected. We pass the airport, and after a few more miles, she takes an off-ramp and pulls onto a frontage road. We're surrounded by sugar beet fields.

"Hold on, I gotta check the coordinates."

I have no idea what she's talking about, so I wait, content to watch the little furrow between her brows as she inspects the map on her phone. Every so often, she glances out the window and then back at her screen.

She sets the phone on the console. "Okay, I think we're

almost to the park." We pull away from the trees and back into the sun.

The park in question is nothing more than an open patch of grass with swings, one pod of playground equipment, and a structure housing picnic tables. A wooden fence separates the field from the park.

"It's hidden near one of the posts, isn't it?"

She grins, her eyes dancing. She really likes the hunt. "Usually there's more walking, but since it's your first time, I went easy on you."

I lift a brow. "Or did I wear you out last night?"

She blushes, but her tone is wry. "Busted. That's totally why."

We get out and she heads for the fence and continues until we're in a ditch between green, leafy sugar beets and a gravel road. I swat a mosquito. The breeze is strong enough to keep this from being a sweat fest. The longer we walk, the more run down the fence gets. She periodically checks her phone.

"Are you getting a signal out here?"

"They wouldn't rate this so easy otherwise. I've done a few that took me two full days of exploring." She speeds along, focused on her prize, while long grasses swipe at her pants. "One time, I did one in Oregon that takes you to a cave in the ocean. You have to hit it at low tide."

My long strides keep up with her easily enough. I admire the view. The startling blue of the sky mixes with the multiple shades of green.

"Then there's one in St. Cloud that sounds like it takes a week to get to the cache and back. I'd love to take a hiatus and travel the world looking for hidden treasures."

"If only you didn't need the treasure to pay for it."

"Exactly. I'd have to bring home more than a mood ring

to pay for it. But still, I've been thinking of where I can go when I leave Fargo."

She's getting farther ahead. My pace slowed at *when I leave Fargo*. We just spent the night together and she's talking about moving?

And that's when it hits me. The girl I'm falling for has no intention of staying.

Thirteen

Lia

I kneel down and scrape away dirt that's exactly twelve inches away from a weathered metal fence post. At the beginning, in the park, the posts were wooden, but as we progress, they've turned into metal ones that are significantly older.

My trowel scrapes along a surface that's definitely not dirt. "Oh! Here it is." I don't care how simple this find is; this is always my favorite part. The whole point of the trip is the find.

I manage to find the edges of the box and lift it out. The dirt's been churned enough recently that there's little resistance.

Ford kneels next to me, a granola bar open in his hand. He's been quiet the whole trip, but then I've prattled on and on about all the locales I'd love to try my hobby at. "Are they always buried?"

"Not always. Sometimes, they're in tree trunks, tucked

between rocks, or even underwater, like that cave I mentioned. Have a seat. Part of the fun is going through the swag."

Ford sits and I take a spot next to him. We both lean over our find. He sifts through the trinkets while I dig out an emoji bandage, my pen, and my own granola bar.

"So, you want to travel?"

I smile wryly over the small bin. "You got the hint, huh?"

"Didn't your parents go anywhere?"

"We used to take vacations and stuff. I miss that, but that's not the kind of traveling I want."

"How do you mean?"

I slip the bandage into the box, sign the logbook, and shut the lid. It gives me time to think about my answer. There's a difference, but I've never had to express it before. "I like to travel with a purpose. Ironically, that's the only time my parents didn't have an agenda. When we went to Cabo, it was to lie on the beach and relax. When we flew to Paris my senior year, it was to eat at cafés and go to museums. Sometimes, they just booked a suite at a luxury resort and pampered themselves." While I died of boredom.

"You wanted to explore more?"

"No. Well, yes. I wanted the treasure at the end. A reason for doing what I was doing. Museums are okay, but their purpose is education or enrichment. I had enough of that in school and I don't know how many fundraisers and holiday parties I've gone to at museums and art galleries over the years. I want to see the world from ten thousand feet, and not just to fly to Paris and back. I want to see the mountains and...I don't know. I want adventure but with a purpose."

His gaze is steady, the blue of his eyes almost neon under the sun. "You ever think about being a flight paramedic?"

"You mean like with Great Plains Life?" I open my granola bar and take a bite. Ford and I have talked before. We've talked about regrets and our past, but this time it's different. I get to tell someone what I want to do. My dreams. "I guess I haven't considered it."

"But you've thought about becoming a paramedic." He says it like it's a given, but I haven't. My life has done a complete one-eighty in a short amount of time and I'm only starting to catch up.

"I'm finally stable with a good job. I'm at a point where I can start thinking about what I want to be when I grow up, and it's a great feeling to know that I can be anything."

"What do you mean? You moved and took the EMT course."

"Yeah, but the course was an accelerated one. A quick and easy way to earn decent money. Plus, I always admired the crews we hired for the big fundraisers. One time, when I was in high school, a guy dropped from a massive heart attack at a campaign rally. The paramedic was on him in seconds. When Mom's team followed up the next day, they got the report he'd survived. I never forgot about it. That and my grandma's nursing tales must be why the course intrigued me."

"Is being a career EMT what you want?"

"Mmm...maybe. It's versatile and I enjoy it." I chomp on my granola bar, taking off nearly half of it. Good thing I bought the slightly gooey ones that're easy to chew or I'd risk choking. "Plenty of people are career EMTs."

"With a little more schooling, you could be a paramedic. Just as versatile and you'd be great at it—and get paid more."

"Maybe. I want to take my time and decide what I really want to do in life. Mitch has been on me about the paramedic course, too."

"I'm not on you about it, Lia. I'm just asking what you want for your future. I'm not planning it for you."

I sigh, releasing the tension that's been building since he started this conversation. "I know, sorry. Mitch isn't the only one that's mentioned it. The boss sent me an email about it, too."

"They don't run the course every year. I'm sure they don't want you to miss out. The company would pay for it."

"I'd have to sign on for three years if they pay for it." I couldn't afford to cover the cost on my own. I give him a playful shove with my elbow. "Then we wouldn't be partners anymore. I'd have my own EMT to boss around."

The corners of his eyes crinkle. "You think you'd want to be partners with me for twenty more years?"

"You think you'd want to be a career paramedic?"

His humor fades. "Like you said, it's a good job, and I'm finally stable."

Ford and I are at the same point in our lives. Both of us were flipped around and had to scramble to make a living. Is he asking me what I want for my future because he's thinking about his own? "Are you certain your chance to get accepted to a residency has passed?"

"I've been out of med school for three years, Lia." Resolve fills his voice and I want to hit him with the tiny flyswatter someone left in the swag bucket.

"Aren't there spots in nearby towns that you can apply for? Grand Forks? Bismarck? Here? You'd get to be close to Jayden and it wouldn't be as competitive." I've never pressured Ford about his residency. Cass did that enough.

That doesn't mean that I think Ford has to throw away his entire medical degree. He enjoys being a paramedic, but I can tell that it's not enough. His mind is always working, anticipating what the ER physician will do once we leave. I know because I've asked him. *What will the ER physician do?* is a question guaranteed to start a long conversation that expands my own medical vocabulary in the process. But when I learned how hard Cass was on him, I stayed away from the residency subject.

He loves medicine, but he's too limited in his role as a paramedic.

"It isn't just that. I was matched with a prestigious pediatrics spot—then turned it down."

"A mediocre residency would still get you in the door." His jaw turns to granite and I clasp his hand. Did I look this stubborn when he was questioning me? "Being a paramedic is an awesome career—not one everyone can do. Just make sure it's what you want."

I can't read the expression that comes over him then. In a flash, he covers it with a grin that doesn't reach his eyes. "Ready to head back?"

"Not until you tell me what this talk was really about."

His brows lift. Confirming that he wasn't just asking out of mild curiosity. "I guess I was wondering if you and I could actually date. Would we work out?"

My mouth opens, but only a little squeak comes out. We haven't been doing this "friends with benefits" thing for all that long. He's slept at my place twice and I hung out with him and his kid once and he's asking if we could...what? "Like date for real?"

"Yeah. Maybe. I mean, we don't have to." His gaze searches mine. "I just thought... I don't know what I thought." He snorts. "I'm not exactly experienced at this part of dating."

"You'll have to elaborate because you know how sad my dating history is."

His mouth hitches up. "If you'll excuse my inner fifteen-year-old, I mean, asking a girl to go steady."

"Go steady?" I giggle more out of nerves, but a spike of delight ignites my belly. "Like, we're exclusive?"

"We're already exclusive; we're just not a couple." He winces. "That sounds weird."

"Backward," I agree with a smile, but I sober quickly. "I'm not looking for the white picket fence, Ford, not yet. Is that what you're wanting?" It's what he had planned with Cass. Only unlike me with Samuel, he was all in.

"With the right person, yeah. As long as she's happy with not-a-doctor Ford."

I could be happy with just plain Ford. This last year, being his coworker transformed my life. I went home after my EMT classes wondering what the hell I was doing. When I got a job, I felt moderately better about my decision.

Then, during my first month as Ford's partner, we responded to a car accident. Getting a patient strapped to a backboard in the pouring rain while Fargo's finest directed traffic around us on a busy highway confirmed my decision. I'd never felt so alive, so useful. Adrenaline pumped through my veins, my heart pounded, and my brain spewed out all the pertinent information I needed. Checking the ABCs—airway, breathing, circulation—how to stabilize the *C* spine, even introducing myself. It was all there, and as we walked out of the ER, soaked to the bone and elated that we'd made it on time, Ford gave me a simple *good job* and I was hooked.

I was hooked on the work but also on the independence. I'd earned that good job—no family connections, no one paving the way. It was all me.

"Not-a-doctor Ford is pretty amazing."

"So are you, Lia," he says softly.

He tilts his head down and I lift my face to his. His kiss is tender at first, then more demanding, turning to all-consuming. Heat licks through me that has nothing to do with the sun and everything to do with the man beside me.

We do work well together, but after our talk, I suspect we don't want the same things at this point in life. Yet when his lips are on mine, I can't bring myself to care.

∩∩

Ford

She's heaven in my arms. I don't care that we're in the middle of nowhere, sitting in the dirt with tall grasses surrounding us. I also don't care about the giant red flag she threw up during our talk, one my mind is busy blocking behind a wall of rampant lust.

We had sex all night long and another quickie this morning. Yet the aching erection straining against my jeans makes me feel like I haven't been with a woman in years.

I draw her across me until she's straddling my lap, her knees spread wide until I'm snug against the part I want most, though it's hidden behind two too many layers of clothing.

Delving my tongue into her mouth, I grip her hips and rock into her. My butt hits the edge of the fence post and I shift us so I can lean back while she rides me, fully clothed. She whimpers and wiggles her ass. If my eyes were open, they'd roll back in my head. I need to hear more.

The urge to drive her crazy hounds me. I don't know why I need it so much. It's not my out-of-control desire and need to have her now. It's more. A confirmation that she's here with me and that maybe I'm not being foolish in wanting her to settle. She has the whole world in front of her and I want her to settle here, with me.

I didn't get that confirmation.

But I can't stop. She's in my arms, and for now, that's

enough. I rip my mouth off her lips and plaster hot kisses down her neck. We're out in the open. This path isn't public, but I won't risk exposing her to any unsuspecting eyes. Doesn't mean I'm ready to douse this fire that's started.

Wedging my hand between us, I find her zipper. I wasn't doing the digging, so I'm free to use my clean hands for the dirtiest activities.

"Ford."

"Just this, Lia." Extreme delight slides through me when I discover her pants are elastic. Yesss. "I have my treasure right here and I want to play with it."

"Oh God," she groans. "You're naughty."

With that simple statement, I know she's never done anything like this under the summer sun.

My fingers find her drenched center. I growl and nip her neck. "You're so fucking sexy."

She circles her hips, anxious for release. I take a quick peek down each side of the trail. Assured we're alone, I slow down and slide my finger back and forth between her labia, teasing her clit with each stroke.

"Ford, what the hell are you doing?" She grinds down on me, yearning for more.

"Just enjoy it. We don't have to rush. No one's coming." Lia's a good girl. Doing it in public is scandalous, but she wants this. I can give it to her without the risk. Even if there's a Peeping Tom with binoculars, he won't see more than us making out.

She briefly pouts, but it turns into a moan as I circle her swollen nub. I string out her pleasure, male satisfaction tightening my gut. I'm the expert on her body. No one else.

She's rocking, straining, trying to get off and I won't let her. The longer the wait, the bigger the release. She needs me to finish and my inner caveman wants to claim her so hard that she can't think of doing this with anyone else. To claim her so hard she'll never leave.

Her gasps are getting shorter and her legs quiver. At last, I thrust two fingers inside and slide my thumb over her clit.

A shout escapes her as she goes rigid. She throws her head back, the sun making her hair gleam until it looks like I have an angel in my arms.

"Oh my God, Ford!" Her shout is carried away by the wind. Fingers dig into my shoulders and I ease the hold of my other arm as she arches back, wet heat flooding my hand.

When she sags, I withdraw my hand and gather her against me. "I've got you."

"I'm jelly," she groans into the crook of my neck. "How am I going to hike back after that?"

"I'll carry you," I murmur against her hair.

"You would try, too."

"Do you doubt me?" Watching her fall apart in my arms has left me with a metric ton of lust to burn off.

Helping her stand, I wait until she's steady before I rush through the quickest burial this geocache box has ever seen. She's shrugging into her backpack by the time I stand. I put mine on backward so it's over my stomach and turn around.

Waving to my back, I say, "Hop on."

She doesn't move. "You're kidding."

"Nope."

"No. Just no. It's not a short walk."

"I'm dying here, Lia. If I don't carry you, I might take you in the dirt." I look over my shoulder to show her how serious I am. I won't attack her, but I'm hurting and I miss her weight on me.

"If you get a hernia, I'm going to be an anonymous caller and vanish before the ambulance arrives."

"Deal."

She's ginger about crawling on, but I hitch her legs up

and she twines her ankles together. I start at a walk and pick up my pace.

"Seriously, you're running," she shrieks and clings tighter.

Yes, I'm running. All those hours on my days off working out with the firemen after Cass dumped me are paying off.

I don't trip or stumble the entire way. Her breath in my ear is my accelerant. I want her breathing heavy and wrapped around me but facing the other direction. And her car might provide enough shelter to make that happen.

We near her car and she digs her keys out and hits the unlock button. I don't drop her at the driver's door but round the back instead.

She slides down my body as I open the door behind her, and any blood diverted from my dick during that run rushes right back.

"I can't believe you did that." She's out of breath, her cheeks still flushed with her orgasm.

"Fireman fundraiser. We used to do stupid relays with the firemen to raise money. You're much lighter than a dude in gear. Get inside."

Confusion passes over her face. "In the back seat?"

I let my expression speak for itself.

Her mouth forms an *O* and she scans our surroundings. All is quiet. There're only the faint sounds of traffic coming off the highway and I'm willing to risk a little exposure. Is she?

"Only if you want to."

She looks around again. "Is it naive that I thought after high school no one messed around in cars anymore?"

"All I'm thinking about right now is that there's a car we can mess around in." As soon as possible. My zipper has to be pulsing with my heartbeat.

Resolve sets in her eyes and she drops her pack on the ground. She opens the door and crawls inside, then spins to shimmy out of her pants.

I grin and bring out my wallet.

I withdraw the condom and toss the wallet on the front seat. I cover myself in record time and crowd in with her.

Since it's my ass in the air, I have to leave the door open, or there's no way we'll fit in her little sedan. It takes some adjusting and shifting before one of her legs is between the front seats and her other foot is pushing against the back window.

She's practically pinned in place by the time I slide into heaven. Sweltering heat grips my cock and I hang my head, letting the bliss wash over me.

I have to use my hands to keep my weight off of her so she's not crushed into the car door, but she's there with me, pushing in to meet my thrusts.

It shouldn't be so hard to see to her pleasure but I have to force myself to slow down and find the angle that drives her crazy.

We're sweating within seconds, but it doesn't slow us down. Her face is red from the warm interior of the car. Before I drip all over her, I open her door and catch her before she flies out the back.

The breeze whisks inside and she braces herself so I don't thrust her out the door.

"Fuck, Lia," I say through gritted teeth. I can't get enough of this woman. I couldn't wait to drive back to town and take her on her bed, where she'd be comfortable, and my ass wouldn't be in the wind. But here I am.

She widens her legs as much as possible and arches her back. The move drops her head until she's looking at the world upside down. Her knuckles are white from gripping the frame of the car door and she releases a throaty laugh. "I can't believe the things you get me to do."

This girl. Drives me fucking crazy. How the hell did I ignore how sexy she was for an entire year? Some part of me must have known that she'd tie me up and leave me at her mercy.

Her breath catches and she tenses. She's going to come. I wedge an arm under her waist to tilt her hips and pound into her.

"Ford!" She comes hard, her legs snapping around my waist like a bear trap.

I'm a goner. I let the ecstasy crash over me, my body jerking against her as I release harder than I can remember.

All I want to do is collapse on top of her and hold her, but we're exposed in so many ways.

She's limp under me. I nip her chin and murmur, "You okay?"

"I'm more than okay. But I'm going to have the pattern of my upholstery tattooed on my legs."

I chuckle and pull out, briefly closing my eyes at the shot of pleasure. I back all the way out and study our surroundings. Nobody. I find the empty granola bar wrapper in my backpack and use it to wrap around the condom, then tuck my dick back into my pants.

Lia's dressed and standing next to me by the time I'm done.

I pull her to me and plant a long kiss on her lips.

When I pull away, she looks up at me through her lashes. "What was that for?"

"I like kissing my girlfriend."

Her eyes flare before a shy smile crosses her face. "I like kissing my boyfriend." We look at each other for a moment. She breaks the silence. "How did we get here so fast?"

"You were untouchable and then you weren't." I shrug. "Maybe being friends first is the key."

"I think so. So now what?"

"We date and have fun." And try very hard not to think about what comes after.

Fourteen

Lia

I get out of Ford's car and skim my fingers under the hem of my sundress to make sure it's not caught in my underwear. I've been out of the dating game for a while, but I wasn't this nervous when I met Samuel at the country club.

Ford and I are on a date—out in public. We aren't pretending and we're no longer friends with benefits. We flew through those stages straight to dating. Each time I think about that quick decision on the side of a dusty road, my insides warm until I glow. We are into each other.

Ford comes around and offers his arm. His white polo hugs his muscles and his khakis adore his ass. I keep trying to walk a step or two behind him to check him out. I've seen that ass naked, but I can always look.

The parking lot behind the restaurant is half-full, but I doubt Tuesdays are a big date night. Ford and I work this weekend and he picked up a shift on Friday. Ford opens the door for me. A hostess greets us with a wide smile and takes us to a table overlooking the vineyard. He orders a bottle of wine after we're seated.

"I've heard this place is nice."

He's about to answer when a woman says, "Ford?"

We both look over. It takes me a moment to recognize Karoline. She's not in a wedding dress, but long, wide-legged pants and a loose shirt. Sergei stands next to her, his arm around her waist.

"Karoline." Ford's tone is neutral.

Karoline smiles and she looks at me. "Hi, Lia. We never got a chance to officially meet at the wedding."

I nod and glance at Ford. The evening started so pleasantly. I hope it ends the same way.

"Sergei," he says evenly. "Nice to see you again."

Sergei nods and awkward silence descends. I call on my old skills of idle small talk. "How was the honeymoon?"

Karoline's face lights up and her smile widens. "Oh, it was wonderful. We've decided to keep the magic alive with weekly date nights."

"We figured we'd better before we start having kids," Sergei said. "I heard it gets busy then."

A server nears the table with the wine and hesitates. Karoline glances over. "Oh, I'm sorry. We're interrupting."

"Would you like to join us?" The words leave my mouth before I can think about my invite. My gaze pops to Ford. His jaw is tight, but I'm probably the only one who notices.

"Oh...do you mind?" Karoline's so innocently hopeful I know it's the right decision. The girl Ford grew up with has matured. She looks at Ford, waiting for his final approval.

"Not at all," he says and rises. The hostess and the server arrange for two more settings.

After we're all settled, Karoline fiddles with the edges of her black cloth napkin folded into a swan. "I'm glad we saw you before we were seated. I keep chickening out of calling. I figured you didn't want to hear from me."

I'm relieved she's addressed the elephant sitting on our table. None of us wants our date night to be filled with uncomfortable chatter. If it's going to go south, it might as well tank right away.

"I..." Ford's brow crinkles as he figures out what he wants to say. "I'm trying to forgive and forget, but forgetting's not easy."

"It's impossible for you to forget. Just know that looking back as an adult, I'm ashamed of the way I acted. Ryan feels the same. I want to keep apologizing, but I'm determined to prove myself through actions. We are not our father."

Ford gives her a begrudging smile. "I did some hurtful things too."

"I think you were a saint given the situation, but you did try to diagnose every sniffle we had. Remember when I refused to go to school because you said my infected bug bite could be the plague?"

Ford's grin is instant. "I'm a little better at that now. I'm sure it was only a flesh-eating bacteria." Before the laughter settles down, I'm brainstorming topics to avoid more awkward silence, but Ford is there first. "Lia and I were at Mom's and she brought out the picture albums."

Karoline covers her face. "Oh no. I've managed to keep Mom from showing Sergei my unfortunate denim phase in high school."

Ford chuckles. "I think your mom almost hugged mine when she talked you out of the denim prom dress."

Karoline's laugh is louder than the rest of ours. "And Ryan kept trying to talk me into it." She lowers her voice. "He was such a shit. I can't wait until his kids are teens. He's going to get paid back so hard."

Over three courses, Ford's shoulders visibly relax as Karoline and Sergei regale us with stories of Ryan's kids, their honeymoon, and life as newlyweds.

When the meal wraps up, Sergei secures the bill. Ford opens his mouth to argue, and I can guess why, though he'd never say it out loud. Karoline's in banking and her husband works for an architecture firm. He doesn't want them to think he can't afford to pay for everyone on his paramedic wages.

My opinion of them rises even higher when Sergei puts a polite hand up, stopping him before Ford can get a word out. His golden eyes are kind. "Please. You have made my wife very happy tonight. Ever since I met her, she's talked about you and wanting to reconcile. Let me treat you and your date tonight."

"Next time, it's on me."

Sergei grins. "Anytime. Anything you two need, call us, please."

Karoline puts her hand on Ford's arm. "Yes. Even if you don't need anything, call, text, or send smoke signals. Whatever works." She turns her megawatt smile on me. "It was so good to finally talk with you, Lia. Can I get your number so I don't have to bug Ford for it later?"

I am ready for the usual round of "Let's do lunch" promises that everyone knows will never materialize into actual lunches, so it takes me a second to regroup. "Yeah, sure," I say, fumbling for my purse. Just as I dig my phone out, a message notification pops up on the screen. Samuel.

Just checking in on you. Everything going okay?

I haven't forgotten him, but I stare at the screen only for a moment before clicking away from it and exchanging numbers with Karoline.

We leave the restaurant and walk out into the mild evening. Warmth kisses my skin even as the sun fades below the horizon. Karoline waves as she and Sergei peel off toward their car. Ford puts a hand on my back. "Everything all right?" he murmurs.

I think about how to answer his question and whether it'll be any different than how I'll answer Samuel's. "Samuel sent a message asking how I was doing."

Ford opens his car door for me and trots around to the driver's side. "He still wants you," he says after he gets inside.

"It doesn't matter." Maybe Samuel's dreaming of me at night and all the ways he could win me back, or maybe he's reconciling with his ex-wife, or maybe he's even hitting the dating scene with someone new—it doesn't matter. "I don't want to get back together with him."

"I think you made that point when you moved to a different town and changed careers."

"Ugh, seems dramatic when you say it like that. The jilted bride, leaving town to start fresh and find herself." I stare out the window at the passing trees and couples out for an evening stroll on the walking paths, on their way home before it gets too dark. "All over a guy. Next time, a man is *not* going to be behind any of my decisions—not where I live, not what I do for work, nothing." No one but me.

Ford's quiet for a moment. "Did you tell him that?"

"No. I'm going to ignore the message. Just because he asked doesn't mean I have to answer."

"Moving to another state didn't dissuade him. Maybe you should tell him how you feel. Don't let him get his hopes up only to then go on with your life like he doesn't mean anything." His hand is clenched on the wheel and the relaxed mood from earlier is gone. His gaze bores into the road.

"I packed my bags and moved out of his house, and the

one time he tries to come and win me back, I showed you off. My part in not getting his hopes up is done."

Tension eases out of him. "I know. I guess I don't know how to react to some dude hitting up my girl. This is new."

"It's new for both of us."

He nods and there's no more discussion as he drives us back to my place. The words we've said roll around in my head. Ford's not the jealous type.

We said we wanted to date and see where things went between us. Are we already going in different directions?

Ford

"Da. Daddy."

I roll over and eye the wide-awake toddler in the portable crib by my bed. He didn't sleep nearly as long as he was supposed to.

"What's up, buddy?"

Jayden jumps up and down and reaches for me.

I swing my legs over the bed and haul him up. "Food, and then we'll figure out what to do for the day."

So far, my first overnight with my son is going okay. Lia came over last night but opted not to stay over. There wasn't anywhere to put her. She wouldn't be comfortable sleeping in my bedroom with Jayden until she got to know him better, likewise for my son.

So it was just him and me last night. Other than the bedtime sippy cup debacle, where the only sippy cup Cass packed wasn't the one he wanted, the night went really smoothly.

In the kitchen, I grab the cup I used to calm him instead

of the offensive sippy cup and fill it with apple juice. Setting him in the new high chair I bought because feeding him on my lap was getting too cumbersome for both of us, I start some toast for breakfast.

I send a picture of Jayden covered in jam to Lia.

My alarm clock.

Two hours go by before she replies, *Cute, but you set it too early.*

The corner of my mouth hitches. I don't mind. Just like I don't mind that my girlfriend can sleep all morning while I clean house and Jayden follows me with a small dust rag.

My girlfriend.

Not only do I have a girlfriend, but I spent the weekend with my kid, and earlier this week, I reconnected with my stepsister. The dinner with Karoline and Sergei was a welcome change from any other date I've had. Karoline even invited us to a cookout with Ryan and his kids next weekend.

I hope I can bring Jayden. Neither Karoline nor Ryan has met him yet.

Jayden rubs his eyes and I glance at the time. It's too early for a nap, but he also didn't sleep on his own mattress. He's growing tall for a toddler and my sleeping arrangements for him are getting cramped.

If he continues to sleep over, I could get a little bed for him. The bedroom I had as a kid is free. I'm storing some old furniture items for Mom that she didn't want to bring to her apartment. I haven't used them in the last couple of years. They could go. Then Jayden would have his own room.

I could even decorate the walls. Something Jayden would like. My gaze touches on the Paw Patrol toys on the floor. He loves Marshall. A fireman. I huff out a laugh. Figures.

A list runs through my mind. A toddler bed. A small dresser. I shouldn't need a changing table since he'll potty train soon enough. I'll have to clear out the closet so he has a place for his toys.

A bedroom all to himself. He has one at Cass's house, but this would be at my place. His own space with me.

The idea snowballs until I pack up Jayden to head to the store. I call Lia. "Want to come with me?"

"Sure. To do what?"

I chuckle. "You agreed before you even knew what I was asking?"

"Hazard of being your partner. I trust you. Besides, Mrs. Rosenthal made another comment about my flower beds and I'll feel less guilty ignoring them if I'm gone."

"Or...you could plant something."

"I keep people alive, not plants."

I don't have to worry about surprising her with flowers then. "I'm going to redo my old bedroom for Jayden. Cass isn't picking him up until before supper. I have time to run to a couple of stores."

"Sounds fun. Pick me up?"

Fifteen

Lia

Ford squats next to Jayden, his hand protectively on the boy's back while they look at various toy storage options. With each piece of furniture Ford picks, he goes over it with Jayden. I doubt many toddlers have this level of input in their bedroom design.

Ford is far more concerned about each choice than his son. Jayden wandered from bed to bed, trying to get into each one and barely looking at any photos of the ones that weren't built for display.

He straightens and swings Jayden up on his shoulders. The boy giggles and clutches his father's hair. Ford winces, but his mouth is tipped in a smile. He's been loving this afternoon.

"It's settled," he announces. "He likes this one."

I eye the set of multicolored bins arranged in two different rows tucked into a wooden frame. People mill around us. The store isn't busy for a Sunday and we blend with the rest of the shoppers. We're just a normal couple, out grabbing a few things for a kid's bedroom. We're not pretending, we're not trying out a real date, and we're not out in nature away from everyone and their prying eyes.

It's nice. This is the normalcy I craved when I moved.

I put my hands on my hips. "It has a fire engine on it. Are you going to allow that?"

"Cops and firemen get all the glory. Besides, I lost the battle when Cass introduced him to Paw Patrol. I think it was a calculated maneuver."

"So we have a place for toys, a bed, and a dresser picked out." Two dressers, but the room isn't that big and Jayden's clothes are pretty small. He didn't have much at Ford's place, but our basket is full of shorts, shirts, and bib sets. We even have a little plastic plate and silverware combo with an array of sippy and regular cups. All Jayden approved. "The big question is, how are you going to get it home?"

Ford hangs on to Jayden's feet and shrugs. "I'll have to see if they deliver."

Something Karoline said the night we dined together comes back to me. "Doesn't Ryan have an old pickup from high school?"

"I think so."

"Why don't you call him?"

Ford stares at me. Jayden wiggles on his wide shoulders, breaking the trance. "I can't call him out of the blue just to ask to use his pickup."

"It'd be good if you reached out for once."

"I'm doing that cookout. We're doing that cookout."

I level him with a hard stare. "Families do things for each other." He opens his mouth to argue and I talk over him. "Not just you doing stuff for them. They want to be a part of your life. Right now, your life needs a pickup."

He lifts Jayden down. "I'm sure delivery is fine."

"Call him, Ford." He needs people on his side. It's been him and his mom for so long. Karoline's been trying to reach out and according to her, so has Ryan. The cookout next weekend is a nice step forward, but Ford needs to learn that he has people around him for more than just small talk.

He scowls at me but takes his phone out of his pocket.

"Come here." I hold my hand out to Jayden and we wander into the next aisle. Ford's voice drifts toward us, but I can't make out the words.

I murmur with Jayden, keeping my voice down, marveling over how I'm wandering around a store with my boyfriend and a kid. It's far from where I was supposed to be in life right now, but this time around, it's *my* journey. My life isn't planned in infinite detail, scheduled to optimize every minute.

My life has changed. Some days, I still don't know what I want to be when I grow up. And at times like this, when I can go where I want with whom I want, I don't care.

Ford rounds the aisle, full scowl in place. "He's happy to help and will be right here."

"He sounded actually happy to help?"

His scowl turns playful. "After he got over his shock, yes. He's bringing his girls."

I ruffle Jayden's hair. "You get to see your cousins, little dude." Despite Ford's words, his shoulders are tight and his hands are stuffed into his pockets. "It'll be fine. Ryan seemed really happy to see you at the wedding."

His jaw works and he glances around. We're alone in the aisle. "I just don't want this day to get ruined. I'm having a good time."

Asking for help when you're always the one coming to the rescue might be a hard change, but there's more here. I think back on the conversations we've had about Karoline and Ryan and what it was like growing up with them. I've heard the stories, I've heard his frustration with the two siblings, but I get now what the issue is. Both kids are older than him and he was only nine when his mom remarried. "You looked up to him."

He lifts a shoulder. "We were just kids."

I grab his hand and lower my voice. "Do this for yourself. And for Jayden. He gets to have more family than just Cass's. Both of my parents are only kids. I have no siblings or cousins, but whether going to the lake or hauling new furniture to your house, it all sounds like fun."

He lifts Jayden and we start for the front doors to meet Ryan. "Our house used to get chaotic at times. Karoline and Ryan were best friends one minute and mortal enemies the next. Add in me and we could get rowdy."

Now that Ford's in a better place with Cass and Jayden, the good times from his childhood are resurfacing more. He's not the only one in a better place. Fargo fits me more than I thought it would when I ran here a year ago. Maybe someday I'll look back on my own early years with a little less resentment too.

∩∩

Ford

Ryan gets in behind the wheel of his old Silverado. My nieces clamber into the back. They doted on Jayden like he was a tiny rock star and my kid loved every minute. Older kids fascinate him; older kids at his beck and call are even better.

The bed was put together and the dresser anchored to the wall. The toy chest was filled with a few extra toys, ones that I didn't buy but that Hallie and Megan insisted on once they were in the store and met their little cousin.

Ryan's window is down, giving me a chance to tell him one more time, "Thanks, man."

"Anytime. You coming over this weekend?"

I duck my head. "That's the plan."

"Lia and Jayden coming too?"

"Lia is. I'll have to see if I can bring Jayden."

Concern mingles with annoyance on his face. "If you need any help with that, I have friends who've been down that road."

That road, meaning custody battles? But there're two sets of ears listening intently in the back. "I'll let you know."

"Keep it in mind."

My initial instinct to brush off offers like that stalls. Custody battle. It's a line I couldn't afford to cross before. But my financial state now isn't as dire as it was three years ago. I have student loans that are getting whittled down each month, but I don't need to help Mom anymore. This house is paid for and my job is stable.

Ryan pulls away and I wander into the house. Lia's stretched out on the rug on the floor while Jayden plays with his Duplos next to her.

I lean against the doorframe and take a moment to soak up this scenario. Jayden was one of the reasons I never let my dates get close, but I couldn't imagine keeping Lia at a distance. She's a natural with him. Not overly pushy, but she never ignored him. She cared for him because he was mine. "You can say 'I told you so' now."

"I'm just glad it didn't backfire. Megan and Hallie are sweet."

"Yeah." I lower myself next to her and run my hand along her back. We keep our PDAs down in front of Jayden.

But being around Lia all day and not touching her is getting old.

I soak in the quiet. Jayden's chilling after the little nap he got while ten-year-old Megan rocked him in the living room and Ryan, Lia and I put the room together. Eight-year-old Hallie hung up decor that she insisted was perfect for Jayden even though they'd just met.

"I hope he can come with us next weekend," Lia says quietly.

"Me too." I've been anticipating Cass's moods and how and when to ask her about the cookout. She took the weekend off for some self-care, so tonight might be the best. Or I could wait until the day is closer so she doesn't have time to change her mind.

Frustration ripples under my skin. Not knowing when I get to see him next and what I can do with him is getting old.

The minutes tick by, but after the busy day, the quiet is soothing.

The doorbell rings.

"There's Mommy." I swoop Jayden up and go to answer. Cass waits on the doorstep, her skin and hair glowing from all her pampering at the spa.

"Hi," she says brightly, her gaze lifting behind me to Lia, her expression remaining neutral. "How'd it go?"

"Good." It's on the tip of my tongue to tell her about our day, but I hold back the details. "He should be worn out. We did a lot of running around today."

Her brows lift and she takes Jayden from me. "Oh?"

Lia comes next to me and hands the overnight bag to me. "He was so good at the store."

Surprise lifts Cass's brows. This is the first time I've done more with Jayden than just watch and entertain him.

This was the first weekend we did normal family things together. "You did some shopping?"

"Ford wanted—"

"I thought I should have some extra clothes here for him." I don't mean to talk over Lia. The bedroom isn't a secret, but I'm hesitant to tell Cass. Telling her that I'm making room for our son shouldn't affect anything, but... what if it does? "Here, I'll help you load up."

"No, I got it." Cass takes the bag and slings it over her other shoulder. "I have my system. Say bye to Daddy."

Jayden waves to us and I watch them go. Cass straps him into her little red SUV and tosses the overnight bag on the floor. She gets into the driver's seat, puts on large aviator shades, and drives off. I wave just in case Jayden's watching us from his rear-facing seat.

Lia doesn't move from my side the entire time. "You don't want her to know about the bedroom?"

I step inside and shut the door, but my gaze burns into the wood, my mind working. I don't regret getting Jayden's room ready. If I don't get to see him much, I still won't undo the work I've done.

But there's no reason he shouldn't be at my place, using his room. There's no reason I can't have more weekends filled with family that supports me and my kids. More weekends where it's my girlfriend sleeping over even when my son's also sleeping over. Days and nights when I take Jayden to Mom's to swim and get grandma time. Times when he just comes grocery shopping with me.

There's no reason time with my son should be dependent on what Cass approves of in my personal life.

My biological father had no interest in me or my life, and my stepfather didn't think I was worth getting to know that well. Jayden needs to know that I'll fight for him and that no matter what the outcome is, he's worth it. My son will never have to prove he's better than me. I'll never make him feel like he's failing some bogus test from a deadbeat stepdad. But I can't make that happen by debating when the best time to ask Cass to see him is.

"I think it's time I check on custody."

Sixteen

Lia

Nerves ripple through my stomach as Ford parks in front of a stucco flat with brick-red trim. Bikes lie on the front lawn and there's a green and black soccer ball in the bushes that flank the front door.

"You look like you're ready to bolt." Ford cuts the engine and we sit outside Ryan's house.

"I'm not." I'm lying. I enjoy being around Ford's family. But I've only met them each once, one at a time. This is a large group of people who have a long history.

I've been to tons of functions with large groups. Those were a huge part of my life. But I didn't have a history with any of them. I was primed to say the right things. I told politicians, reporters, and donors what they wanted to hear and that was that. They forgot me as quickly as I forgot them.

I can't do that here. I don't have a statement to read from, talking points to hit or a script I'm required to recite.

Whether it's telling reporters about the platform my mother's running on, or telling a patient I'm Lia from Fargo EMS and I'm here to help, I knew what to say.

I don't know what to say today. These people are important to Ford. I like them. And if things between Ford and me keep going the way they are, they're going to be part of my future.

"Mom's coming, but I don't see her car here yet."

"I wish we could've brought Jayden." Cass's parents have a conference in Minneapolis, so she's driving there to visit and taking Jayden. Of course.

A cloud crosses his face. "Me too. But I got him last weekend. I'll promise Karoline to call her when he's over next so she can see him."

Ford's gaze flicks beyond me a moment before someone knocks on the window.

I jump, my hand flying to my heart. I thought I had nerves of cast iron, but today is proving that wrong. I swivel around in my seat. "Mitch?"

His wife, Samantha, is standing next to him, grinning and holding a container with what I hope is the famous brownies she brought to last year's company potluck.

I open the door and Ford leans over to ask, "What are you doing here?"

"Samantha used to watch Ryan's kids in her day care, remember?"

I faintly recall Mitch mentioning it once, but that was back when Ford purposely avoided anything relating to Karoline and Ryan—which was any time before two weeks ago.

Ford and I get out and walk to the door with Mitch and Samantha. Laughter filters through the house from the backyard.

Karoline opens the door and claps her hands. "Hello,

everyone! Come around the back. We have lots of food." She eyes the tray Samantha's holding. "I told you not to worry about anything, but I'll forgive you if they're brownies."

Samantha brandishes the tray. "I'm forgiven."

Karoline takes the tray and waves us to follow her.

Mitch falls in step beside me. "We get any more people from work here and we can just have our company picnic at Ryan's."

I laugh as we enter the backyard and my anxiety fades. An inviting aboveground pool twinkles in the middle of the yard and sits empty except for the girls' pool toys floating on the surface. A trellis full of vines surrounds the patio and provides protection from the sun. Sergei's talking to Ryan. When they see Ford, they both call out greetings. Sergei adds, "Glad you could make it."

Ford and Mitch meet them by a cooler and I follow Samantha and Karoline to a picnic set up in the shade.

"Name your poison," Karoline says while Samantha and I get settled. "I've got water, sparkling water, lemonade, spiked lemonade, iced tea..."

"Lemonade. Want help?"

"No, sit and have fun. I'm going to shoo Ryan's wife, Rosa, out of the kitchen before she cooks anything else. We'll have leftovers for a year."

Samantha's rueful smile turns toward me. "She's not exaggerating. Rosa lives in fear of food running out on guests." She digs a pair of sunglasses out of her purse. "So, how've you been? Mitch tells me you're thinking about the paramedic program?"

I am? "I guess he mentioned something, but I haven't really thought more about it. I like what I'm doing. I feel like I have a lot to learn."

"Trust me, it's easier to do your schooling before the marriage and the kids come. And you'd still be working and learning while you're taking courses. You know the company will pay for it."

"If I sign on for three years."

Her gaze slides to Ford standing with the group of guys by the grill. "Are you planning on going anywhere?"

A question I've pondered recently and have a firm answer for. "No. Not at all."

"Then you have nothing to lose. Except Ford as a partner."

Right. I'd have my own EMT partner once I became a paramedic. Is that what's stopping me?

That question deserves time. I let a guy sway my future once. I'm not doing it again. "Ford mentioned Great Plains Life."

Samantha nods. "Mitch considered becoming a flight paramedic." She chuckles. "But he hates flying, so... You'd be good at it. He speaks so highly of you."

I like my job. I enjoy flying. Can I mix the two and still love them both? My gut says yes. Not only does it feel right, but if I take the course offered through work, then, like Samantha said, they pay for me and I can keep working. A few years after that, I can work toward becoming a flight paramedic if it still feels right.

My gaze is drawn back to Ford. He's laughing at something Ryan said, his broad shoulders shaking. I'm not letting a guy influence my decision, but I like the thought of being around for a while. Of having a future with him.

As if he senses me thinking about him, his eyes meet mine, the blue in them catching a line of sun that found its way through the vines. The corner of his mouth hitches up and I match his small smile.

He nods like I've given him the affirmation he was looking for. I'm doing okay. More than okay. I wish I could go back to the brokenhearted Lia from after the breakup, the one who looked at a map on her phone and wondered where in the world she could rebuild her life. I wish I could tell her that she's making the best decision of her life. That she'll find herself and in doing so, she'll find a real partner.

∩∩

Ford

"Want something to drink?" I wander into Lia's kitchen. The place is dark. We haven't turned on any lights yet. Ryan's kids went to bed well before the party wound down and Lia invited me to sleep over. Since watching her all night and not being able to touch her was a special form of torture, I most definitely accepted.

My hand is raised to flip on the light when she says, "Leave it off."

I like the sound of that. "Tell me you're naked already."

Clothing rustles in the dark. "Now I am."

"That's what I've been waiting for all day, baby." I rip my shirt over my head. "Get on the table."

She hesitates.

I undo the clasp on my pants. "The table, Lia. I'm a starving man."

"You're so naughty," she breathes but pads softly to her small kitchen table. A chair scrapes against the floor.

I grab my wallet before I drop my pants and walk out of them. After I have the condom, I toss the wallet and don't care where it lands. She's leaning against the table, not on it like I asked, but I don't care. I'll make her comfortable enough to perch on it and spread herself for me.

But first, I have a question.

I approach her, not saying a word. Her breathing quickens and I'm as hard as a rock, yet I take my time.

When I reach her, I don't attack but drop my head and capture her mouth. She snakes her arms around me, aligning our bodies in the dark until my erection is smashed between us.

I let the kiss linger until our lips break apart. I keep my voice quiet, preserving this moment between us. "Not that I'm complaining, but what prompted you to jump me?"

"I didn't jump you."

She can't make out my dubious expression. I've always been the initiator of the first round. After that, she's my wanton little goddess, but tonight's different.

She runs a hand along my collarbone and up my neck. Cupping my face, she says, "I'm just really happy right now. I like where I'm at and who I'm with."

"Good. Because I don't plan on going anywhere." A flood of relief cascades through me, going so far as to dampen the stiffness of my hard-on. We're both on the same page. We have the same goals. Other than chemistry and respect, that's become one of the most important things in a relationship. Something I've avoided until now. Until I found the right person.

The moment of relief is over and need pounds into me. I need to claim her, make her mine, again and again, until we're both too boneless to move from each other's side.

I grip her ass and lift her to the table. I love the hitch in her breath, the way she's always surprised that I can handle her so easily.

Feeling behind me, I find the chair and take a seat, moving her legs apart as soon as I'm settled.

"Ford—"

I go in for a taste. There's too much desire in her tone, too much longing, she's too close to begging. This moment is proving something to the both of us. It's like a promise. Me and her against the world.

Her head drops back. Her hands are planted beside her and they keep her stable as I lick her over and over, fast then slow, just the way she likes.

"I can't hold on—" She tries to muffle her cry, to keep from waking Mrs. Rosenthal next door, but it's a lost cause as she comes on my tongue. I haven't even used my hands or any other part of my body. Just the tip of my tongue and she's mine.

I rise, hooking her legs around my waist. She collapses back, breathless. "I don't usually come that fast."

"You will again," I promise.

I get the condom on, but everything else after that is unhurried. We have the rest of the night with each other.

I slide my thumb through her folds and rest it against her clit. She gasps but arches into me, caught between wanting to draw away from being so sensitive and needing to get off again.

"I've got you." Slowly, I push a finger inside. With only the motion of my finger going in and out to move my thumb on her swollen clit, I build the next climax one tiny thrust at a time. Once the sensitivity of the first orgasm is gone and she matches my movements with the surge of her hips, I speed up and add little circles.

She's spread out before me, her beautiful breasts just out of reach while I strum her body. Soon. I'll get to those, but she comes first *in all ways.*

She draws her knees up, her climax close, and I watch her intently. It's dark, but I can read her moans and the frantic way she's rolling her hips, seeking her release. As she crests, I remove my finger, leave my thumb on her clit, and shove inside.

Her body clamps down on mine as she cries out, not

bothering to cover the sound this time. She rides my dick and I force myself to remain still as she finishes.

When I sense she's almost done, I let myself go. She's molten around me, all wet, tight heat and it doesn't take long before my own climax slams into me, nearly toppling me right over her.

I catch myself with my free hand and move my other hand enough that I'm not rubbing her too-tender flesh. I sag overhead, still inside.

"Fuck, Lia. I love getting you off."

She wraps around me and brings me close enough for a kiss. "I just so happen to like it too."

I nibble her lips until I feel a stirring, a coiling that I've come to associate with Lia. I pull out and pick her up. The condom can be dealt with after I carry this treasure to bed. I have the rest of the night to show her how much she means to me.

Without her, I wouldn't have had the extra time with Jayden or the confidence to reconnect with my siblings. I wouldn't have nights like this, ones when I don't have to search for my clothes in the dark and creep out of some strange house or hotel before I'm asked for more than another orgasm.

This woman means the world to me, and with any luck, we've got many, many more nights like this to come.

Seventeen

Lia

I jump into the shower to wash off the day. Ford and I took Jayden to Maggie's house and helped pull weeds in the complex's yard. I got more than a little dusty but managed to keep streaks of mud off my face, unlike both Ford and Jayden.

Jayden's spending the night at Ford's. Another overnighter for the pair. I'm thrilled for them. I was also invited, but since he hasn't told Cass about the bedroom yet, I declined. Best to leave things as uncomplicated as possible until he has custody secured.

I've just finished getting dressed when my phone rings. One look at the display and I groan.

Mom.

Why can't she be more like Maggie? Ford's mom is so laid-back and accepting. She sees the world through a "How can I help you?" lens instead of "What can you do for me?"

I love my mother. I just wish she was more Mom and less State Senator Elaine Wescott.

"Hello." I slide between the covers. It's too soon to go to sleep and I haven't eaten, but this conversation is going to exhaust me.

"Aurelia. I'm glad I caught you."

I work three twelve-hour shifts a week. She rarely fails to "catch me." Is she insinuating that I should be doing more with my life, that I should be busy when she calls? "What's up?" Because I know she didn't call to chat.

I pick at a loose string on my comforter. I have to remember that I can't change her. I can't change Dad, either. They love their lives. They love their jobs. It's not up to me to make them understand that I want the same, but different.

Mom's breath hitches. Something's coming and I'm not going to like it.

"We have the annual fundraising gala coming up."

I chew the inside of my cheek. I missed last year's. I had just started my job and refused to ask for time off to go work the crowd and avoid Samuel. I didn't trust myself. Resisting him a year ago would've been next to impossible.

Funny how when I think of him now, the panic I used to feel at the thought of encountering him is gone. We have a lot of history and the future I planned to have with him was one for the ages, but that's evaporated as thoroughly as last week's rain shower.

Encountering him again is going to be uncomfortable. He's messaged twice to check up on me and I've ignored him both times. Any interaction we have will be uncomfortable. Ford's right. I should've stopped avoiding him and confronted the situation.

"I'd like you to come," she says after I don't immediately reply.

I don't want to go, but I also miss them. I can change my life, but a part of me will always be that girl striving to live up to Mom and Dad's expectations, wanting their approval. After the way things at the country club went, I should refuse to attend. But by now Mom must realize I'm not coming back home and she still called and asked me to come.

I pull up my schedule. "When is it?"

"A month from Saturday. I know it's short notice, but I don't think you'll have trouble finding a dress."

"I'm not working." And that means neither is Ford. "Will Ford be welcome?"

"Aurelia..."

I bite my lip. The sting of physical pain takes my mind off the hurt. Did she only ask me to get me in the same room as Samuel? "Mom. Samuel and I are done. I've moved on."

"Ford's a nice-looking young man. I'm sure he was a perfect rebound, but honey, you and Samuel... He's been relentless for so long. I've heard he hasn't been dating or—"

"Dating isn't the same as having sex, but neither one is any of my business. We're done, Mom. You need to accept that it's my choice." I roll my lips in. I don't usually challenge my mother. Having lawyers for parents should've made me an expert debater, but it's only shown me how futile it is to continue with someone who's determined to be right no matter how wrong they are.

"Your father and I have had a good life."

"Okay?" This isn't the turn I was expecting in the conversation.

"We..." She lets out a gusty sigh. "We started out much like you and Samuel."

I stare at the abstract pattern in my blankets. Colors swirl, eventually mixing together to make a distinguishable picture. Unlike the pattern, I can't make out what the hell Mom's getting at. "What do you mean?"

"Before we were married, we broke up. Much like you and Samuel."

I snort. "Did one of you cheat? Because otherwise, it's nothing like me and Samuel."

Her answering silence fills in the blanks.

I gasp and sit up straight. "No. Who?"

"Me, Aurelia," Mom says tightly. "And it was a mistake. I was young and insecure and I didn't make the same mistake ever again. Your father forgave me and we've been an unbeatable team ever since."

It all makes sense. Mom's ashamed of what she did. A mistake that must have happened nearly thirty years ago. What happened between me and Samuel has brought it all back, has exhumed all her feelings of shame and guilt and betrayal. "Do you think that if you can save me and Samuel, it'll make up for what you did?"

"Of course not. But I know exactly how one stupid mistake doesn't have to destroy something beautiful. You and Samuel were good together. He's genuinely remorseful."

"We're not you and Dad." They're committed to each other. Whatever happened in the past, they realigned their goals in life and met each one. Infidelity wasn't the straw that sent the camel crashing down.

"Aurelia—"

"No. I'm glad you and Dad made up, but I'm not Dad. He loved you enough to work things out. Samuel might seem like he wants to work things out, but he didn't love me, not really. He loved the person both of you thought I should be."

I don't want to be a mini Elaine Wescott or follow in Gerald Wescott's footsteps. If I had been true to myself in college, I wouldn't have fallen for a guy like Samuel, likewise for him. He thought he was getting a young woman with big political ambitions who would do whatever he needed to make it happen, two-point-two kids and all. I'm not her.

I wasn't strong enough to stand up to Samuel. I ran to a small town that I knew none of them would follow me to, at least not for my sake. I wanted to surround myself with people who supported me instead of expecting that my only role in life was to support them.

I can stand up to both Samuel and Mom now.

"What are you talking about?" Mom hasn't reached the epiphany I just did. "You were head over heels for him. That's why what happened was so devastating. I understand that. I've been trying to help you see that you're a strong girl, and together, you two can get through this."

"I am strong, but I wasn't then. Mom, I don't want to be a lawyer. I don't want to be a judge or run for public office. I don't want to follow my parents around, and definitely not my husband. If I never see another reporter, it'll be too soon."

"You always did evade the spotlight. I could barely get you on stage for your school plays."

It's enough to coax a smile. "I like what I do." I like being there when I'm needed the most and moving on. Let the doctor get all the glory. I don't need it. Just my own slice of paradise in Fargo.

She sighs. "Are you saying that you didn't run to the first little town you could afford to live in and take the first job you saw in the paper that would earn you a half-decent living?"

I cringe. I might accuse her of being Senator Wescott more often than not, but she can still catch me off guard with her mom senses. "Maybe it worked out so well because it called to me."

She makes a noncommittal noise. I don't have to convince her. I only have to convince myself and I'm more determined than ever to steer my own life.

"I don't love Samuel. Not anymore. I think he's a great guy, but we didn't work."

"Aurelia." She lets out a long, slow breath. "I can see that now. But are you sure this Ford is right for you?"

"We're figuring that out and we're doing it together and it's working really well."

"I guess I'll have to live with that. Well, if you two are still together in a month, feel free to bring him." There's the distrusting lawyer slash senator I know and love. "If he's comfortable at this type of thing."

"He's done a lot of galas before with his ex."

Ford must be rubbing off on me. I never would've brought up that part of his life before. She'd consider it a weakness and use it against him.

I'm not worried. My parents will approve of Ford, or they won't. It doesn't change my trajectory.

"The ex with the kid?"

"Yes. He feels the same way about galas as I do." We'll suffer through them because they're important to someone who's important to us.

"You'll be punctual this time?"

I think back to Ford's sudden turn and our meandering trip to the country club—and how things turned out afterward.

I guess there's only one way to find out.

ᑎᑎ

"Maybe it was something you gave him?"

I level Cass with a steady stare. Jayden hasn't been feeling well, and he's had one suspicious runny diaper. Just before his mom showed up, he said his tummy hurt. "It wasn't anything I fed him. I'm sure he picks up all sorts of germs at day care."

Cass plants her hands on her hips and tilts her head, her blond hair shifting to cover her face. Her hair is down today, there're bags under her eyes, and she's stressed, like she's spoiling for a fight. I assume two things. One, that Jayden didn't feel good last night and that's why it looks like she didn't sleep more than four hours. And two, that she's gonna take it out on me to make herself feel better. Typical Cass.

"Are you saying that I don't take him to a quality day care?" Her voice is rigid.

"No, I'm saying that he runs around with a bunch of kids all day who put their hands and mouths God knows where." Since I caught Jayden trying to chew on the bottom of my shoe last night, he's included in that statement.

She pushes the fall of hair off her face. "Fine, it is what it is. I'm sure it's nothing." She scans the house, her blue gaze calculating. "No Lia today?"

I was ready for her to berate me for being a horrible dad, but she's moved on to the bad boyfriend material. It's a more familiar route.

I keep my answer simple. Lia isn't always here when I have Jayden. "No."

"Seems to be working out." Her tone is soft, her question sincere. It's enough to throw me off.

"We haven't been dating long, but it's going well." Silence falls between us. I don't know what she's looking for.

Jayden's playing behind us. There're no banging sounds like normal when he plays with blocks. But he's sitting among his toys, halfheartedly touching a shiny mirror here and flipping a plastic bobble there. I wouldn't mind if he made some noise, something to distract Cass from taking her bad mood out on me.

"Is Lia going to be happy being stuck in little old North Dakota, doing nothing but acting as your sidekick?"

Is that what Cass felt like she was during our engagement? My sidekick? I thought we were a team. When I told her that Mom needed help and I had to move home, we had an epic argument, but then we decided to move forward as a team when she followed me to Fargo. Then, when she snagged a position in hospital administration, I thought we were set.

I didn't know that she'd moved with me to create some distance between her and her parents' opinions of us and our baby on the way. Just like I didn't know until it was too late that she thought our move was just a temporary pause before we moved on to bigger and better things. I failed, and she punished me.

I'll never forgive her for leaving me off the birth certificate. But she stayed in Fargo. All I can do is move forward and play nice until I figure out exactly how to approach the custody issue.

"Like I said, this is new. She's not planning to leave."

"I guess you were just waiting for a girl who'd settle down. I can understand that after what we went through."

I recoil like she's slapped me. Where did that come from? She thinks I played the field until I found a perfectly compliant girl?

I clench my jaw to keep from saying something that'll set me back several months. Broaching the custody topic might do that on its own. It's been a long road, and I've missed a lot with Jayden, and I need to make sure that doesn't happen again. Her parents might not have agreed with her move here, but they'd jump on taking legal action against me. I'd get incinerated fighting Cass for custody.

She watches me for a couple of seconds like she's expecting a reply. What does she want, an acknowledgment that, according to her, I fucked up? Profuse apologies for moving her to my hometown and trying to provide for my family?

Won't happen. I did what I had to do and she took my son from me as punishment. One thing my actions did was show the glaring weaknesses in our relationship and bring me to Lia. A woman who understands and supports me.

Her eyes fill with resignation and she shifts her gaze to Jayden. "Ready to go, pumpkin?" She walks to him and squats down, feeling his forehead. "He's a little warm. Did you take his temp?"

"He was warmer than usual, but not enough to qualify as a fever."

"You're the doctor," she mutters. No one refers to me as a doctor. It's like they all sense what a sensitive subject it is and stay away from it. The term is a reminder of a life that won't ever be mine to live. I shouldn't be surprised Cass is the one to wield it against me.

Cradling Jayden to her, she rises. He whines and squirms, and she murmurs something comforting. I turn to grab the diaper bag when a horrible retching sound fills the room.

When I spin around, my eyes widen. Jayden cries and he tries to pull away from the mess he's vomited all over Cass's shirt. Cass's mouth is hanging open as she holds him away from her.

"Ford!" she shrieks.

I grab Jayden. I hold him facing out so I don't get covered in vomit. "Go clean up. I'll change him." There's an extra outfit in the diaper bag.

She holds her arms out, afraid to move and spread the foul-smelling substance. "Yuck." Her chest heaves and she looks down at herself, her expression growing more horrified by the second. "Gross. What the hell am I going to change into? I can't drive home in this."

"Go find one of my shirts."

She looks at me, trying to comprehend my simple words while she's dripping in kid vomit that's on a whole different level than spit-up.

"Go." I snag a disposable baggie from the diaper bag and wave it at her. "Put your shirt in that or leave it here and I'll wash it."

She nods numbly but reaches for the baggie. She disappears into the hallway and I carefully strip Jayden down so I don't smear the bits that hit him. After I change him, I take his temperature again. Holding steady, nothing to worry about.

"Hopefully this passes quickly, little man." I pick him up and he drapes himself over my shoulder. I'm not as worried about getting nailed with puke. Just concerned that he might throw up again and be sicker than I fear.

There's a knock at the door. I rub Jayden's back on my way to open it.

Lia's on my step, wearing aviator shades. Her pink shorts show off her long, tanned legs and the baggy T-shirt makes her look young and carefree.

She pushes the shades up and I'm impressed that they can hold back her thick hair. "Hey." Her nose wrinkles and she looks around for the source of the stench. "How's it going?"

"Not the best. Sorry for the vomit smell."

Her brow crinkles and she looks beyond me, the corner of her lips pulling down.

I glance over my shoulder and my stomach sinks. *Fuck.*

Cass has emerged from the hall. She's swamped in one of my old college T-shirts that brushes the tops of her knees.

The baggie holding her dirty clothes—both her pants and top—hangs from her fingers.

The problem isn't that she's in my house, wearing only my shirt. The smell alone explains everything. Lia will understand why I didn't send Cass away full of puke.

No, the problem is that Cass is staring into Jayden's room. "When did you do this?"

"Oh." I exchange an *oh shit* look with Lia. She steps into the house next to me. I'm going to need her support for what comes next. "Cass, there's something I'd like to talk to you about."

∩∩

Lia

I don't want to be here right now. This moment screams private, something a new girlfriend, hell, even a good friend, should sit out.

Ford's been agonizing over how to approach Cass, whether or not to go to a lawyer first or test the waters and see if she's receptive to the idea of compromising on arrangements.

Cass crosses her arms, the shirt hitching up on her thighs. Her haggard appearance isn't just from Jayden's mess. I don't have time to ponder before her voice cuts through the moment.

"Okay." Her voice is full of challenge.

"We can talk more later. This obviously isn't the best time," I try.

Her gaze jumps to me, then back to Jayden clinging to Ford. "What is it?"

"I'd like to discuss joint custody arrangements with you."

Her expression frosts over and her gaze oscillates between me and Ford. "You two have been planning this?"

My gut clenches. The ice shards protruding from that question are more than ominous. Everything Ford feared is unfolding. Cass doesn't want to lose control. It's all she has over Ford.

I want to cling to his arm, to rub my hand on Jayden's back. He has to sense the tension between his parents. But I remain still.

"What do you mean?" Ford asks.

Cass waves her hand between us. "This. I accused you of being a poor role model. So you're making this perfect little family with a perfect little room to be happy forever."

Ford holds a hand up. Cass falls quiet, but she blinks tears back. His brow is crinkled. Like him, I don't understand the magnitude of Cass's reaction. Does she feel like we're teaming up against her?

"I don't understand, Cass. I get what happened between us. I get what upset you so much, but I don't get what you mean about planning this. I mean, we still live in the same town. You stayed and you got a good job. What have I done wrong now?"

She sighs and rubs her forehead, then grimaces and pulls the hem of her shirt down, suddenly self-conscious. "Nothing. Sorry. It's just been a stressful week and now I have a sick kid. I should get him home and get him cleaned up."

She marches over and holds her arms out for her son. Ford shifts Jayden to her hold and he curls into her like she's holding the cure to his tummy issues in the borrowed shirt.

"I wanted a space for Jayden to be comfortable here. The portable crib is getting too small."

"No, I get it. I overreacted." Her smile is wan. "Like I said, hard week. Anyway, thanks for watching him."

She scurries out the door and Ford helps her load Jayden and the diaper bag.

I stay out of sight, unwilling to add to Cass's rough week so she can take it out on Ford.

He enters the house and lets the door shut behind him. "So that was weird."

"I'm glad you sensed it." I don't know why Cass would find Jayden having his own room at his father's house so personally insulting. It's better for Jayden than camping out every time.

"I don't think she's going to voluntarily sign the declaration of parentage."

I shake my head. "No, not if seeing a bedroom made her react that way. What's next?"

"Court order to establish legal parentage. It could get ugly."

"You do what you have to do."

He nods, stress etched into his chiseled features. He scrubs his face. "You said you had to talk to me about something."

I grimace, not wanting to heap more onto him. "How do you feel about flying to San Francisco and renting a tux?"

Eighteen

Ford

People in formal attire mill around us, going in and out of a tall set of double doors. On the other side, a giant ballroom teems with laughter and soft classical music. Everything about this place screams money and prestige, from the red uniforms the doormen are wearing to the coattails on the tuxes the cocktail servers are wearing.

I adjust my tie and Lia sends me a bemused glance.

"It's tight," I mutter.

"I'm sorry you can't leave the first two buttons open like your work polo," she teases.

Her comment eases my tension only slightly. "Was this how you felt when you came to the cookout?"

"Not having to take two different flights or wear a tux made it a little easier."

"I didn't think it'd matter." I have a case of nerves like I've never had before.

When I met her parents before, I made a point of *not*

impressing them. I don't want to alienate them tonight. Lia and I are a real thing. I support her. I always will, but no matter what happened between her and her parents before, she still loves them.

She doesn't have to say it, but she still wants their approval.

And because of that, I'll be on my best behavior.

It helps that this trip to San Francisco is a temporary reprieve from custody worries. I haven't gotten more than one weekend with Jayden in the last month. I don't know what's going on with Cass but she evades all my questions and requests.

How could redecorating one bedroom cause that?

I shove it out of my mind. This night is for Lia. Who knows when I'll ever be in a tux again, and I want to enjoy the way she looks in her shimmering dark-red dress. She's piled her hair on her head in a simple but artful style that took her all of fifteen minutes.

"Practice" was all she said when she left the bathroom of the hotel and my jaw hit the floor. Her long, graceful neck is bare and so are the shoulders that first caught my eye in the country club. The dress she found loves her curves as much as I do, and the slit on the side is going to gnaw at my sanity all evening.

I hold my arm out. She smirks but hooks her hand around my elbow and I lead her inside.

We're right on time. I made sure of it. There's no devil-may-care Ford tonight.

It's not hard to guess where her parents are. A large group of people are clustered in the center of the room.

I'm striding toward it, thinking of proper ways to break through the throng of people to get Lia to her parents, when a familiar voice comes from our left.

"Aurelia."

I would've ignored Samuel, as he's not the reason we're here, but Lia's grip on my elbow tightens, slowing me down.

"Samuel, hello." She manages to sound cool. Collected.

His jaw tightens. "Ford, right?"

"Nice to see you again." I extend my hand. My willingness to impress doesn't extend to him, but I'll take Lia's cues and be polite.

He shakes it, then turns back to Lia. "Senator Wescott said you might make it. How was the trip?"

"Ford drove, so it was easy for me. We just arrived, so I have yet to greet them."

Samuel glances over his shoulder, where I have yet to spot Elaine and Gerald Wescott. "The party reps are here, vying for her attention."

"I know how it goes, and I'm glad I don't have to deal with it anymore. If you'll excuse us."

I take that as my cue to steer us away from her ex, but as we start, he reaches a hand out.

"Wait, Aurelia. Did you get my—" His eyes flick to mine. "Mind if I talk to her privately?"

Lia shoots me a questioning look. She has unfinished business with the man and I hope she takes this moment to tie off a loose, dangly end. But that's not my decision. If she wants a word with him, so be it.

I incline my head. "Want something to drink?"

Samuel answers instead. "Refreshments are on the far end, but there are servers with trays of the moscato she likes."

I arch a brow. I didn't come here to piss on his territory.

Instead, I ask Lia directly. "What would you like to drink?"

Lia bites her lower lip like she's trying not to grin. "Thanks for asking. Water is fine for now."

I don't bother giving Samuel a dirty look, leaving to get what my woman says she wants.

I dodge chatting couples and small groups on my way to the minibar. Next to it is a table holding flutes of what I hope is water. I grab one, and at the same time, a server wanders by. I do what I've seen in the movies and grab a glass as they pass.

"It's Aurelia's favorite," a woman says next to me.

Mrs. Wescott.

"This is for me, actually. She wanted water."

"Mm." She tilts her head like she's inspecting a bug, but her expression is more curious and less hostile than I expected.

I lift my glass toward the group of people I assumed she was in. "I thought we'd have to fight our way through there to get to you."

Her smile is brief. "An aide needed a word. Gerald is used to covering for me as I get pulled away." She looks around. "Where is she?"

"Samuel wanted a moment."

Her brows lift. She's an older version of Lia, just as elegant, but with an obvious command of power. I can see how the woman's shadow swallowed Lia up. "Indeed. And you're okay letting her go?"

"She can make her own decisions. She doesn't need me to make them for her."

Mrs. Wescott nods. "I'm surprised you came. After our last meeting, I didn't think you'd want to."

And if I didn't, neither would Lia. "We do things that are important to the people who are important to us."

Mild surprise registers in her expression. "These things haven't been important to Lia."

"But they are to you, and I can't speak for her, but I think she misses you."

This time her smile is sad. "I miss her as well. Her father does too. I suppose we could make more time to travel. We just thought…" She purses her lips.

"That she'd come back."

She feathers her fingers over her tight bun. "I suppose every parent's goal is to raise their children to make their own way in life. I shouldn't complain when she does just that."

"She's amazing at her job."

"Indeed. I shouldn't be surprised. Gerald's mother was a nurse and she used to bend Lia's ear with stories. I didn't think she remembered them."

"They must've been close." My phone vibrates. Dammit. I ignore it.

"That they were." She pats my suit coat over my phone. "You're buzzing, Mr. Monroe. I'd better let you go, but I'm glad we had his chat. Make sure Aurelia finds us as soon as she's free. She'll know how to cut through the crowd."

I plan to ignore the call anyway, but she slips away. I weave to a corner of the room by a side panel the servers hustle in and out of, setting down our glasses on an empty serving tray.

My phone is done ringing by the time I fish it out. Cass.

Frowning, I call her back. "Hey, what's up?"

"Ford, I didn't expect you to call back so soon. I stopped by your place."

"Is something wrong?"

She pauses and I turn my back to the room like it'll help me hear better. "I have to talk to you about something."

"I've got a few moments." I don't, but she's never dropped by to tell me something. My gut says this shouldn't wait.

"Oh no, we should meet in person—"

"Cass, I'm out of town. What's going on?"

"I was offered a position at a hospital in St. Paul. I accepted."

Air whooshes out of my lungs. My world stills and all the noise behind me fades away. "What?" I couldn't have heard her correctly.

"It's more pay, more staff to help with the workload, and I can even work from home a day or two a week."

"Cass...St. Paul? That's...that's not—"

"Not Fargo? I know. But it's better for me and Jayden."

Jayden's better nearly four hours away? "What about me?"

"You can come visit."

"Cass." I can't believe she's doing this.

"Look, Ford. I've thought long and hard about this." She'd said that the last time she ripped the rug out from under me. "I've been applying to different places."

"You went on interviews when I was watching Jayden?" I didn't think she could sink lower than she did the day he was born and she left my name off his birth certificate.

"You're moving on. It's time for me to. I've stayed here for three years for you."

"How can you say you stayed for me when you *left* me?" I shake my head. "You know what, never mind. It's in the past."

"It's not like I could go running home to my parents after leaving like that." Bitterness laces her tone. "Enough time has passed and I have the work experience to go anywhere. It's not far. You can still visit."

"I want to do more than visit. I want to be there for him. I'm his dad." I'm a dad who wants to be around.

"You had your chance. Anyway, I have to give thirty days' notice. We'll be moving next month."

"Cass—"

There's a cry in the background. "We'll talk about this later."

She hangs up and I stare at the phone. When I look up, there's no Lia, no familiar faces. I'm alone in a crowded room and I'm losing my son again.

∩∩

Lia

My arms are crossed across my chest, my fingers clenched around the clutch holding the hotel key and my phone. Samuel hasn't given me a chance to get out what I want to say.

"Then Senator Wescott said—"

"Samuel, I'm sorry, but we're done."

Confusion mars his brow.

I continue before he can tell me more about his latest accomplishments. "My mother can still mentor you without being your mother-in-law. She won't cut you off if we don't get back together."

"This isn't about her, Aurelia. It's about you and me."

"No, because you don't know me. At all. I tried to be what you wanted and what my parents wanted, but that's not me. That's not Lia Wescott. I'm going to be a paramedic. I'm dating Ford. I'm getting to know his son and his family. And while I still might come and do these things if Mom asks, I don't ever plan to touch politics again."

"But..."

I give his bicep a squeeze. "You'll find someone who aligns with you. Maybe it's your ex. Maybe the image you thought you needed to succeed only cost you what you really wanted. I don't know. That's for you to figure out. But you and I?" I point at him, then me. "We're done."

I march away, leaving him stunned silent behind me. There. Dealt with.

I keep walking while searching the room. Mom approaches the large crowd in the center but tilts her head toward the side of the room when she catches my eye.

Ford's broad back is to me, his shoulders hunched.

Concern curls in my gut as I dodge women in heels and men in suits and servers with trays. I hurry as fast as my sparkly heels will allow.

"Is something wrong?" I ask as soon as I'm in range.

He peers over his shoulder and his expression is destroyed.

I round his front, laying a hand on his shoulder, and stare into horrified blue eyes. "Ford?"

"Cass is moving. She's moving to St. Paul and she's taking Jayden with her."

"What? That's awful."

He shakes his head, staring at the floor but seeing nothing. "I can't believe she'd do that."

I look around at the people going about their business, having an enjoyable night while donating money to their party. I haven't gotten to talk to Mom or Dad, but this isn't the place for Ford.

"Let me message my parents that you're having a family emergency and we're going back to the hotel."

My fingers fly through the words before tucking my phone back into my clutch. I thread my fingers through his and we plow through the crowd, out to the elevators. My parents reserved a suite for me, making this trip a lot less expensive than it could've been.

I punch the number to our floor. Once we're inside the

room, I slide out of my shoes and sit on the bed. Tapping the spot next to me, I say, "Sit."

He shrugs out of his jacket and loosens his tie. Sinking onto the bed, he puts his head in his hands and props his elbows on his knees.

"She's fucking taking him away again. *Goddammit.*" He drops his hands and stares at the ceiling, his profile rigid. "I can't let that happen."

"You're working on the court order. Meanwhile, we can research lawyers, and then..."

He shakes his head. "That could take years. Each day that passes, she has more authority. She's the unmarried mother, while I took over two years to establish parentage. It's going to look bad."

"I'm sorry." I rub his back, wishing this night could have been so different. "But you're on the right track."

"No, I'm a failed doctor who's not in his son's life. I'm even worse than my own dad."

"Ford, your dad has nothing to do with this," I say quietly, but it's as if he doesn't hear me.

"I need to move."

"What now?" Does he want a more comfortable chair?

"St. Paul's far enough away that it'll make visitation hard. I can't be an absentee dad. I have to move."

"But... your job and your mom and..." Me?

He stands and starts pacing, his hands on his hips. I'd appreciate the strong lines of his body if his declaration weren't so startling and so resolved.

"I can be a paramedic there. They're always hiring. Mom's doing well. It'll be better in the long run. She'll end up seeing her grandson more if I do this." He nods as he paces. To the door, turn, then to the window.

"I support what you need to do, but what about us?"

He stops and stares at me as if he's just realized I'm in the same room. "We can do long distance."

"Can we?" I don't want long distance. But I don't want to lose him.

"Lots of couples do."

I nod, but something about this situation sits in my stomach like a bowling ball. "But does one of them leave the other to follow his ex to another town?"

His brows drop. "It's for my son." He says it slowly, enunciating every word.

"Cass broke up with you because you refused to leave Fargo. Now she's leaving Fargo and not ten minutes later, you're leaving too?"

"That first decision cost me a hell of a lot."

Emotion swells so high in me that I have to stand and burn it off. "Right, again, I understand. All I'm saying is give it a few days to think about."

"I don't need a few days. Why don't you come with me?"

He says it like it's a simple solution to a complicated problem. "I'm signed up for the paramedic course. I'm locked into three years. My home is in Fargo." Add in the length of the course and we're looking at a *long* long-distance relationship.

He rolls his lower lip between his teeth and considers me. "You won't leave? Not even for me?"

"It wouldn't be for you. It'd be for your ex and I've already done enough for one guy hung up on his ex."

"So, what? You'd just start ignoring my messages?"

Low blow. He's hurting. I'll give him some leeway, but this problem isn't going to be solved unless he stays or I leave. As it stands, neither one of us is budging in our decision. "For your information, I made sure Samuel understands we're through and we'll always be through."

He's quiet for a second before he huffs out a breath. "The night you stand up to him, you put your foot down with me. I thought we were a team."

"A team doesn't mean one person drops their entire life for a spur-of-the-moment decision."

He shoots me a glare that could wither a cactus. "My kid isn't a spur-of-the-moment decision."

I'll never win this argument and I don't know that I should. He needs to do what he has to for his family. I need to do what I have to for me.

My voice shakes as I say, "Why don't you go then? Since I'm here, I might change my flight and stay with my parents for another day."

He stares at me for a heartbeat, his expression hard but stricken. "So that's it then?"

My nod wavers as much as my resolve. "Do what you have to do."

"I'll see if I can switch with Mitch until I'm done."

I nod again, words unable to form on my tongue as tears gather in my eyes. I hug my arms around myself and stare out the window as he disappears into the bathroom to change and pack his things.

Then he's gone. It's like the last couple of months haven't happened. Once again, I'm heartbroken in San Francisco. This time, I have somewhere to go, but when I return to Fargo, I'll be a single woman who lost her best friend.

Nineteen

❧

Ford

I knock on Cass's door. I've had shit for sleep since I returned to town on Sunday. Now it's Monday evening and she should be home from work. The mess of feelings inside me is tangled worse than a hose in a hurricane and I can't sort them out.

I'm desperate. I'm devastated. I'm sick as hell of feeling powerless.

It's been less than forty-eight hours as a single guy and I'm lonely as hell and missing Lia with every fiber of my being. I miss my girlfriend, but I can't even go to work and talk to my friend about it.

I don't work until next week. I managed to pawn off my shifts for the week, calling in every favor owed to me for covering people's asses when I was a single guy with no responsibilities. Jada and the time she was too hungover with a blood alcohol level that was probably too high to even drive legally. Russel, who thinks he's

God's gift to the Star of Life and should've been fired years ago. He almost let an elderly dementia patient leave against medical advice without determining adequate mental capacity until I saved his ass. And Mitch. I just told him the story and he covered the only day he was able.

Cass opens the door, her lips pulled down. "Ford."

"Can I come in?"

She steps aside and I enter. Jayden runs to me and I scoop him up. I could hold him forever, but I have to talk to his mom.

"I'm moving to St. Paul too." Might as well get to the point.

She blinks, then crosses to the high-back seat in the dining room that's right off the entrance. Gesturing to another chair, she crosses her long, tanned legs. This woman used to drive me crazy in all the best ways. Now, it's hard to tolerate being in the same room.

"I'm moving," I repeat after setting Jayden down with a tower of Duplos.

"What about your mother? And your job?" It's not lost on me that Lia asked the same thing. "And Lia?"

"Jayden's my main concern."

She scrutinizes me and I see something I don't like. A spark of hope. "Did you and Lia break up?"

It's my turn to study her. Was this part of her plan? Her ultimatum three years ago backfired, but she stuck around. Then she issued another one, couched in concern for our son. And that backfired. Now she's moving. And here I go, running after her like she's always wanted.

"Lia's staying here," is all I say. "My concern is my son. I'm going to be a part of his life."

Cass leans closer, a small but noticeable move. "You're actually leaving North Dakota?"

There it is again. Hope mingled with just a little morbid glee.

For your information, I made sure Samuel understands we're through and we'll always be through.

I gave Lia some advice once and she followed through. I need to do the same.

"We're over, Cass. If there was ever any chance of reconciliation, you trashed it. Then you trashed it again. My respect for you only goes as far as you being the mother of my son and that's where it will stay."

She draws back, her hand going to her chest as if my words physically hurt.

I don't let up. "I'm moving *for him*. I'm pursuing joint custody *for him*. Whatever there was between us has long since died."

Emotions play across her face. Shock. Anger. Hurt. Disbelief. Resolve. "Doesn't feel good, does it?"

"What?" I ask even though I don't want to hear whatever it is.

Each word's an arrow that punctures the target with cruel precision. "Losing the one you love because they're so damn stubborn."

∩∩

Lia

When I arrive at work on Tuesday, I don't see Ford right away. I spent days dreading running into him again, yet it was the one thing that sustained me through the hours until now. The thought that maybe he worked out a solution where we could stay together and he could see his boy.

But my phone remained silent.

Both of my parents heard the story over breakfast before Dad drove me to the airport. We talked the whole way. He surprised me with all his questions about my work and when the best time to visit is. Then Dad was gone and I started my life again as a single woman flying to a different state. I made the same mistake again. The only people I know are through work and through Ford.

Why can't I learn?

I won't have to worry about that changing. He'll be gone in less than two weeks and I'll be starting my new course. Maybe I'll meet some friends there.

Still no Ford, but Russel Hayes is lingering around the rig I'm assigned.

Shit. Did he switch with Russel? I don't want to be on the douche crew.

Russel lifts his chin when he sees me. "You're with me today, rookie."

Is he serious? "Not a rookie," I call as I go to the locker room to unload my change of clothes.

Back out in the bay, we get updated, and no matter how much I fantasize about it lasting an hour or two, it only takes minutes. Soon, Russel and I are on duty.

"You're driving, rookie."

I roll my eyes and do as he says. When I'm a paramedic, I'm going to use him as an example to my trainees of how not to act.

Our first call comes in right away, saving me from hours of Russel reminding me how to do the simplest aspect of a job I've been doing all year.

"Fifty-two-year-old male struck by a motor vehicle…"

Mentally, I'm scrolling through a list of what could be wrong and what materials we need. As we pull up to the intersection, there's a figure lying by the curb, a small crowd circled around him. Police officers are directing traffic and

Officer Nelson gets out of a second police car and waves us over.

I park and Russel jumps out, leaving me to do the grunt work. Ass.

I haul out the cot with the jump bag secured on top and hurry after Russel. I aim for the patient, but I'm waylaid by a man in his thirties wearing a suit and tie. I keep walking. Unless the man was hit by the car, he's not my priority. I've learned the hard way to get to the patient first. Witnesses will talk my ear off about what they saw while a hit-and-run victim bleeds out.

"I'm a doctor." His offer doesn't make us pause.

Russel's tone is almost bored. "What kind of doctor?"

"Excuse me?"

He sends the man an annoyed look, his chin lifted like a Roman emperor. "What's your specialty?"

"I'm-I'm a dermatologist."

"If we find an irregular mole, we'll let you know."

My eyes flare. Ford's never that rude. To anyone. It's a regular occurrence to have a nurse or doctor stop to help. Emergency medicine may not be their specialty, and they might not even be trained in first responder skills, but at the very least, we politely thank them for the offer of assistance.

"Did you see the accident?" I ask as soon as Russel stomps away.

He rips his frown off my partner and shakes his head. "I heard it and helped him off the road." His lips form an apologetic smile. "He was going for the curb whether he had help or not. I tried to minimize any damage. All doctors do rotations in the ER."

"Will you hang around in case we have any more questions?"

He ducks his head, relief obvious in his eager stance. "Sure, of course."

Confident that we're not going to be called into the boss's office to get reprimanded after Dr. Dermatologist calls to complain about Russel's attitude, I hurry after the arrogant bastard.

So many examples of what not to do with this guy.

He's already asking the patient questions. As for the patient, he wants to leave, and he wants to leave yesterday, but the bulge under his pant leg won't let him. I'm one-hundred-percent sure that he's busted a femur.

The man is swearing and gritting his teeth. Yelling for us to let him go and shouting at the driver, with terrified eyes, standing by the police car. "Just let me go. It's not my fault that bastard didn't watch where he was going."

Ford's usually the calming one, but Russel's talking in short, curt sentences and ignoring me. The rest of the call feels like a fumbling mess as I try to anticipate Russel's intentions. He won't look at me and I only know he's talking to me when he spouts off medical jargon.

I hold in my temper as we drive to the hospital.

Russel ditches me and the patient to go refill his meds, leaving me with the updates and probably all the computer work. The patient's arguing with the nurse and I look for the doctor I need to give my report to.

I've been spoiled with Ford for a partner. For the first time since our hotel fight and breakup, I worry about my decision. Mitch has Arnesh as a partner. Russel's an idiot that should've been fired years ago. There's Jada, who's okay to work with. I scroll through the rest of the paramedics I could partner with until I finish my courses.

I've committed to the company. If I wanted a different five-year plan, I shouldn't have signed that contract. I could've been free to go. I could have been a paramedic in St. Paul. Then I'd also have to pay for my education on top of the cost of the move. They might offer the same contract, but I'd be locked in. What if Cass uprooted Jayden again?

I'd be stuck doing what I did years ago when I let Samuel lead me around, making decisions for me, disguising them as my own. No. I square my shoulders and rattle off the report to Dr. Sanchez.

As the saying goes, I made my decision and I'm sticking to it.

Twenty

Ford

My new apartment is filled with my old things. Until my house sells, I'm on a tight budget. Mom comes out of the bathroom, where she stocked my towels and washcloths. I didn't ask her to help, but she insisted. I asked her to keep Karoline and Ryan out of it. They've been nothing but supportive and have been great resources for finding me lawyers to contact, even offering up the retainer, but for the actual move, I wanted to come and lick my wounds on my own.

She brushes her hands and looks around my new home. "That's about all. When do you start work?"

"Next Monday." I'll be working at St. Paul's Level 1 trauma center. Unironically, it's the same hospital Cass is an administrator at.

"That'll be exciting."

"It'll be something." I have zero interest in meeting my

new partner. Whether I'm stuck with the same person for each shift or rotate, I don't care.

"I'm sure you realize that it's that time of year."

"November?"

"It's not too late to apply for residencies. You're in the Twin Cities, where there're actually spots."

I frown and stare at the swirls in my boring ceramic tile floors. Minneapolis has a medical school and between the city and St. Paul, across the river, I have plenty of options. I haven't thought of residency for weeks. Not since Lia last mentioned it.

Mostly, I just think about Lia. Between her and fighting for custody, I have no other thoughts. They've taken over my brain.

"It's over, Mom."

"Actually, I think it's time to start." She approaches me like she's cornering a tiger. She cups my face like she used to do when I was a kid. "You've done so much for others. Think about yourself. Think about what you want."

"What I want is in Fargo." I can't believe I've confessed that. "But it's also here and I can't be in two places at once."

"Perhaps once you do what you really want to do in life, what you're called to do, the two things will have a way of joining together."

"Life doesn't work that way."

She lets me go and lifts a shoulder. "Then think about what you'd want your life to mean if you don't win the custody battle." She turns away, leaving me reeling from one simple question. "I'd better hit the road so I can get back before dark. Love you, hon."

"Love you," I mumble.

What do I want my life to mean? For so long, it was about being better than my birth father and stepfather.

Then, it was about being a better dad than each of them. Now, both of them are out of my life. I'm fighting to keep Jayden in it, but while I'm doing that, then what?

I wanted to be a pediatrician. I spent my youth working with kids so I'd have the rapport I needed to build such a good reputation that I'd get headhunted for somewhere like Johns Hopkins. And prove to Nathaniel that I was better than him.

I became an EMT to get medical experience and make my medical school application more impressive. I became a paramedic to make a living.

I do more than that. I make a difference. Working at the St. Paul Level 1 trauma center will allow me to do that. But it doesn't call to me. Not like the speed of being in the field, making the decisions.

I can't deny the emptiness inside when I hand off a case to someone with the initials MD or DO behind their name.

I roam my apartment, my mind whirling. Am I just grateful to have something else to think of other than how Lia's doing and how I'm going to afford a lawyer?

I spot the bag with my laptop and stop. I stare at it for a moment.

Shit. I swoop it up and dig the computer out. What can it hurt to look?

∩∩

Lia

My mom stops at the table where my pile of books is sitting. She and Dad flew out for the weekend. She runs her hand along one and opens the front flap.

"ALS?"

"Advanced life support," I answer.

She pages through it. "This is some heavy stuff."

I love learning it. It keeps me occupied. Between school and work, I only think about Ford every other second.

The new year has come and gone and I've heard nothing about him. Mitch looks at me like he wants to tell me, but I don't ask.

A guy like Ford has moved on already. I don't need to hear it out loud. Hopefully he finds someone he can trust enough to start a relationship with.

Hopefully his new partner is a dude.

I can't help petty thoughts. I can't help but hope he's as lonely and forlorn as I am. I should be a better person, but that's the best I can do.

I do truly hope his custody fight is going well.

Mom puts the book down. "No word from Ford?"

I know she's been dying to ask since she arrived last night. Dad's testing out one of the local golf courses, and Mom and I just got back from Mrs. Rosenthal's. I lost at cards again. But I'm learning who my mom really is besides a powerhouse politician.

She's funny. She's sincere. She's invested in who she's talking to. I can see why she's always voted back in. Mostly, I can see that she wants a better relationship with me.

I haven't gotten one Samuel update since Ford and I broke up.

She even went geocaching with me yesterday. I picked a simple one at a local park. It was the first time I'd gone since that day Ford and I had sex in his car where I didn't stare at the cache and think about it every second.

"We're over."

She drags in a breath and blows it out. "Tell me again why you insisted on staying here and not moving?"

I shoot her a hard look. We had such a good day and

now rain clouds are building over my head again. "I told you why."

"Right, but with Samuel, it was because you were living a life you didn't want." She sweeps her arm around the room. "Isn't that what you're doing here?"

I swallow hard. "I'm happy."

"Oh, honey." She takes a step closer. "You're miserable."

"It's too late," I whisper. "He's moved on."

"How do you know?"

"He hasn't called." Total radio silence. He walked out of that hotel room and he was done with me. He even found someone to work his last week. We never saw each other before he left. He made sure of it.

"He's also been hurt terribly before by someone he loved. I imagine he's more than a little gun-shy."

I sniffle around a scornful laugh. "Now you're on his side?"

"I admit he won me over at the gala."

"You never told me that."

She tilts her head. "It wasn't exactly the time."

And this isn't exactly what I want to hear. "What am I supposed to do, Mom? I've started my classes. I've signed on for three years. I'm committed."

She lifts her chin and speaks like the stern senator she is. "I'm disappointed. How can you be my daughter and not realize that every contract can be broken?"

Hope sparks in my chest and I squash it. "I'm sure he's—"

"Yes, moved on. You keep saying that, but you don't really know, do you?" She closes the distance between us. "If you're worried about money, don't be too proud to ask us. We're here for you. We've saved for you. There's a whole fund that didn't get used for law school."

That...would be a lot of money. "I can't."

"Why the hell not? Your father and I haven't worked this hard to let you settle for a future you hate. You can afford to do whatever you want, move wherever you want." She lifts a regal brow and crosses her arm. "Then maybe you can be with whoever you want."

Love isn't the problem. My mom's offer doesn't change anything. Months have gone by and Ford hasn't contacted me.

He's also been hurt terribly before by someone he loved. I imagine he's more than a little gun-shy.

I could do worse than swallow my pride and reach out. I could send him a message like *I've been thinking about you. How are you doing?* God, that's so lame.

Then he could tell me to fuck off since he's against ghosting those kinds of messages.

But then I'd know for sure.

I look for my phone.

∩∩

Ford

I throw on my boots and beeline to my bedroom to change. At some point, I should quit picking up shifts and working overtime. But it's not like I have anything else to do, and I need the money.

The retainer for my case is a fortune and I can't find a lawyer who can help me before my son is ready for college. The house hasn't sold yet, but there's a serious offer pending approval from the bank. I'd like to say I'm hopeful, but the last few months haven't given me much to hope about.

I rub my eyes, toss my phone on the bed, and strip down. It buzzes before I jump in the shower, but I don't bother to look. At this point, no news is good news.

Cass won't talk to me, so unless it's her offering profuse apologies, then I don't care.

I towel off and find a pair of black shorts and a T-shirt. All I'm going to do is sleep in them and change out of them for work in the morning.

I glance at my phone as I walk out of the room, my stomach growling.

The name on the screen stops me short.

Lia. *I've been thinking about you. How are you doing?*

I go back to the bed and stand over it. Wasn't that the same weak-ass message that Samuel sent her once?

I told her not to ignore it but to tell him point blank that he didn't have a shot.

What does she want out of me? I can't tell her she doesn't have a shot. That'd be the biggest lie I've ever told. So what do I do?

I stare at the phone.

I can't ignore it after I told her to tell Samuel off—and then she did.

I can't send a simple message like *Fine*. I'm not fine. Not at all.

I can't...I can't quit fucking thinking about her. I can't quit dreaming of her. I can't quit wanting to tell her about my day or vent about lawyers—I know she'd understand. I can't quit regretting what I did even though I saw no other way.

I can't quit loving her.

So I pick up the phone and bring up a number I've dialed several times before. My boss answers.

"Hey, Lori. Can I take a sick day tomorrow? I'm feeling rough."

I'm not above a little bit of lying.

"No problem, Monroe. You've been working so much since you started I worried you'd burn out. Get some R&R, come back when you're refreshed."

After hanging up, I whip through my room and pack a bag. In a few minutes, I'm in my car and driving. I don't stop until I reach a condo with a neglected flower bed and a nosy neighbor.

♋

Lia

My doorbell rings. It's well past the time anyone with altruistic motives would be knocking.

I rush to the peephole in my flannel pajama pants and oversized shirt, hoping to catch them before they ring again and wake Mrs. Rosenthal.

I can't make out who it is other than a big figure enclosed in shadows. My heart rate kicks up. "Who is it?"

"Ford."

I open the door before the answer registers in my conscious brain. "Ford?"

He pushes in but I offer no resistance. He stares at me, drinking me in in the dark. The last time we did this runs through my brain and I recall every taste, every sensation from that night.

"I got your message," he finally says, his voice rough. His hair is spiked like he's run his hands through it a thousand times.

"Yeah?" I'm breathless.

"You knew I couldn't ignore it."

It's true. I did. "Yeah."

"So, I'm here to tell you I'm not doing well. St. Paul fucking sucks. My job's fine, but I work all the time and the house hasn't sold, so I haven't made any headway with custody. I've also applied for ER residencies and haven't heard back yet."

"Oh. Oh, okay." I nod like this is anything close to a normal conversation. "I'm not doing well, either. I don't have a set partner, so I get paired with Russel way too often and he's such an ass."

Ford drifts closer. "You're part of the douche crew."

"It's awful. But school's going well. My parents have been up to visit."

That makes him pause. He's so close, he's towering over me. "That's good. That's really good." Another step and we're inches apart. "I'm not doing good without you. I don't care, Lia. I don't care that we're in different cities or that you don't want to move. I'll make it work. I'll make it fucking work because I'm so in love with you I'd rather have you a phone call away for years than never have you."

He says everything my dream Ford has been telling me the last few months. Am I still asleep? Is this still my dream Ford? "I realized that I don't really have a good reason to stay in Fargo. And that means I don't have a good reason not to be in St. Paul when I'm so in love with you."

His forehead touches mine. "I don't care where you're at, as long as we're together somehow." He drops his mouth and his lips press mine, increasing in pressure until he wraps his arms around me and lifts me against him.

My back hits the wall. We're on the same page, about to do exactly what we did the last time he showed up on my doorstep late at night.

Our hands are all over each other, pushing and pulling at clothes until we're both naked. He takes his wallet out of his shorts. "I think the condom in here is expired."

"They're usually good for years."

With a slow smile that's big enough for me to see in the dark, he drops to his knees and we make up for lost months together.

Epilogue

SIX MONTHS LATER....

Lia

"I'm telling you, it's real." Karoline hikes ahead of me. The sun's bearing down on us, but she's sticking to the part of the park with copious trees.

I found a beginner geocache. Come with me. I'll get the coordinates. You just make sure I don't get lost and wander the wilderness for days.

So far, we haven't left the city limits. We're on the fringes of the park where Ford and I stopped for cheesecake bites.

I adore Karoline. She's become my best friend while I've stayed behind to finish my training. But I have the weekend off, and so does Ford, and I'm supposed to hit the road soon.

"Oh! Look. I found it."

Since Karoline's standing in the middle of the walking path, I don't think she has. "Are you sure? It's probably buried..."

Awareness shivers down my spine. There's the big tree. There's no blanket. No cheesecake bites. No Officer Nelson.

But there's Ford, looking ruggedly handsome in jeans and a light-blue polo shirt. He's tucked his hands into his front pockets and he's watching me with wary hopefulness.

"You're supposed to be just getting off work." I've been set up. Karoline *begged* me to go with her on her first geocache until I relented, despite knowing it'd cut in on my precious weekend with Ford.

Karoline snaps her fingers, but I can't take my gaze off Ford. "I need to leave something behind, right?" She grins. "That's you." Looking immensely proud of herself, she continues down the walking path. "I'll have my phone just in case, but if my bonus brother does this right, you won't need to call me."

"Are you supposed to be the treasure I take with me?" My feet are rooted in place, more secure than the decades-old tree towering above us. There's something else going on here.

"I got the spot."

I jump off the path and into his arms. He catches me with ease and swings me around. "That's great! St. Paul's newest ER resident. Congrats."

"All that overtime while we were apart paid off. They said they knew before my interview that they'd take me."

"I knew you could do it. We'll be total noobs together." I move down to St. Paul at the end of the year. Long distance sucks, but he's only a drive away and we're both so busy. "Oh, Dad called today. He called a couple of friends and one works out of Minneapolis. He'd be happy to take on your case."

"This day can only get better one way."

"Oh yeah? We're not allowed to make out in the park, remember?"

He pulls away from me and drops to one knee. My hands fly to my mouth. He didn't drive here just to surprise me with his good news. He's right. This day can only get better one way.

Taking a ring from his pocket, he holds it up. From behind me, someone lets out a little squeak and I don't have to look to know it's Karoline holding back a squeal and taking pictures.

"Lia Wescott, will you marry me?"

"Yes, Ford. Of course." I drop to my knees and slam my mouth against his. The ring can wait. I need a little public make-out session with my future husband first.

∩∩

Five years later...

Ford

I bite the inside of my cheek as Mitch's new partner stammers through the report. Arnesh is now a paramedic with his own EMT and I'm back in Fargo. Only I work at a hospital as their newest ER physician.

The poor rookie finishes her report and smiles.

"Thank you. Good work."

She beams and Mitch rolls his eyes. When she walks away to tend to the cot, he leans in. "You can be a little harder on them, you know."

"Nah. That's your job. Got a minute to hang around?"

Mitch nods and leaves me with the patient. I run through the case and rattle off my orders for the nurse. So many new faces and a few familiar ones.

But one familiar one is waiting on me outside the treatment room, talking to Mitch and probably catching up on the latest Fargo EMS gossip.

When I finally finish, I find my wife, Great Plains Life's newest flight paramedic, showing Mitch pictures of our one-year-old girl. Ella Elaine Monroe is the favorite of both grandmas and the bane of her three-year-old brother's existence. But Kellan Ford Monroe can take care of himself and negotiate whatever he wants out of all his grandparents.

Both kids adore their older brother, Jayden, and he has his hands full between them and Cass's twins.

I'd like to say I fought hard for custody, but my lawyer did all the work for half the fees. Gerald Wescott's contact was worth four times what he charged. I've had joint custody for the last four years and once Cass started dating her now husband, she even apologized.

It's not exactly water under the bridge, but Lia and I have an amicable relationship with Cass and her new husband. Which is good since she's going to be my boss's boss next month as the hospital's CEO. She's got her family, I've got mine, and we both have Jayden. The past can stay in the past. Each of us has too much going on in the present.

"Is my wife spreading lies?"

"Now, Dr. Monroe." Mitch shakes his head. "I can't tell you how happy I am to call you that."

"Technically, you could've before."

"And you would've hated me. I gotta go check on the rookie. The whole family going to Ryan's cookout next weekend?"

Lia grins and tucks her phone away. "He's on call, but the kids and I will be."

Five years. I thought I lost it all more than once, but I got more than I could've ever imagined. The woman of my dreams, a house full of kids, grandparents who can't get enough of them, and siblings of my own. And it's all because of this woman right here, wearing a flight suit that can't possibly hide a body I can get lost in for hours.

I spent a lot of time trying not to dwell on why life wasn't working out the way it was supposed to, but I wouldn't have wanted to end up anywhere else *with anyone else*. Everything happened the way it was meant to.

Lia leans in close. "That reminds me. Jayden's with Cass tomorrow night and your mom wants to take Ella and Kellan overnight. We get the night to ourselves and I hear you do this thing with your tongue . . ."

———

If you'd like some steamy small town romance, it all kicks off in King's Crown. Kendall takes a private jet with an oil tycoon to interview with his son, but they get stranded in a snow storm for a few days. And when the weather clears she has to tell the son she's working for his dad instead—and she's dating him too.

For all the latest news, sneak peeks, and FREE bonus content sign up for my newsletter.

About the Author

Marie Johnston writes paranormal and contemporary romance and has collected several awards in both genres. Before she was a writer, she was a microbiologist. Depending on the situation, she can be oddly unconcerned about germs or weirdly phobic. She's also a licensed medical technician and has worked as a public health microbiologist and as a lab tech in hospital and clinic labs. Marie's been a volunteer EMT, a college instructor, a security guard, a phlebotomist, a hotel clerk, and a coffee pourer in a bingo hall. All fodder for a writer!! She has four kids, an old cat, and a puppy that's bigger than half her kids.

mariejohnstonwriter.com

Follow me: